TO HAVE AND TO HOLD

Matt kissed Julie's shoulder, then her neck, soft gentle kisses. "Jules?"

"Mmm?"

"I don't want to get on my bike and go back to Philly and be without you again."

Julie clasped her arms around Matt and held on tightly. "I don't want you to, either."

"Then marry me, Julie."

Julie felt a beat of astonishment. She pulled back so she was looking into Matt's eyes. His expression told her he was as serious as he'd ever been about anything. "We said it one way last night. Let's make it official. Why wait any longer?"

Forever. Julie and Matt. Holding each other. Being there for each other. No more longing, awful phone calls. No more letters that stood in for the warmth of his touch. Julie took both of Matt's hands in hers. They were warm and trembling. The tenderness in his eyes filled her with happiness. "Yes, Matt," she said. "I'll marry you."

TO HAVE AND TO HOLD

First Comes Love

~1~

Jennifer Baker

Cover photo and illustration by Denis Ryan

Point Romance

■SCHOLASTIC

Scholastic Children's Books,
Scholastic Publications Ltd,
7-9 Pratt Street, London NW1 0AE, UK

Scholastic Inc.,
555 Broadway, New York, NY 10012-3999, USA

Scholastic Canada Ltd,
123 Newkirk Road, Richmond Hill,
Ontario, Canada L4C 3G5

Ashton Scholastic Pty Ltd,
PO Box 579, Gosford, New South Wales,
Australia

Ashton Scholastic Ltd,
Private Bag 92801, Penrose, Auckland,
New Zealand

First published in the USA by Scholastic Inc., 1993
First published in the UK by Scholastic Publications Ltd, 1994

Text copyright © Daniel Weiss Associates, Inc., and Jennifer Baker, 1993
Cover photo and illustration copyright © Denis Ryan, 1994

ISBN: 0 590 55623 1

Printed by Cox & Wyman Ltd, Reading, Berks

10 9 8 7 6 5 4 3 2 1

One

❧

"Bye," Julie whispered, but she couldn't turn and leave.

"Bye, Jules," Matt said softly. He didn't move away, either.

Julie touched his cheek with her palm. His skin was warm. She traced the arch of his dark eyebrows over his deep-set gray eyes, the straight, broad slope of his nose, his full lips. She tried to memorize every tiny detail of his face: the faint scar above the inside corner of his eye, the freckle near the side of his mouth. His dark brown hair needed a trim.

"I can't believe this is really it," she said. "Good-bye—it sounds so weird."

"Weird and awful," Matt agreed. He cupped her face in his hands. "I'd ask you to stick around if I thought it would do any good."

Julie glanced over Matt's shoulder. In the driveway behind him, she could see her parents and her twelve-year-old brother, Tommy, waiting for her in their tan-and-white station wagon. All of Julie's things were loaded into the back of the car —suitcases full of clothing, boxes of cassettes and CDs, the brand-new laptop computer she'd gotten for her high school graduation, her ice skates. She was also bringing posters and pictures to decorate her room at college—including her favorite picture of her and Matt, sopping wet and grinning after a day of inner-tubing on the Delaware River. For Julie, the photo captured the spirit of the entire summer. It had been great, probably the greatest summer of her life. And now it was over, and everything she owned was packed into the car. If only she didn't have to leave behind the thing she cared about most of all—Matt.

When she looked back at him, there was no sign of his familiar grin. "Matt, you know I don't want to be away from you," Julie said. "Not for a minute, but . . ."

Matt shrugged. "Yeah, I know, but at least you'll be off in a new place, meeting new people—" He hesitated. "New guys . . ."

Julie frowned. "Stop it. How can you even think that? I've already met the best guy in the whole world, right here in Philadelphia. That's hardly why I'm going." She didn't want to say it out loud, but right that second she was wondering why she *had* decided to go away to college. That morning, with the sun still low and mellow, the grass damp with dew, and the air sweet, her small, neatly trimmed front lawn with its cherry tree and its manicured hedges was the place she most wanted to be—as long as Matt's arms were around her.

Matt gave her a sad little smile. "Best guy in the whole world, huh?" He stroked the side of her face, his fingertips lingering on her lips.

Julie stretched up to kiss him. As she wrapped her arms around his broad back and shoulders she breathed in the familiar scent of his skin. A bird chirped in the cherry tree. A light breeze rustled the leaves and caressed Julie's bare arms.

She trembled. She could feel Matt shaking, too. She had to hold back the tears. "I can't believe this is really happening," she murmured. When she thought about waking up the next morning four hundred miles away from Matt, all her plans and goals seemed to shrink to nothing. Was going to her first-choice college really so important? There were plenty of good schools near Philadelphia. Sure, she'd always imagined that part of college was leaving home—but leaving

Matt was more than she could handle. It didn't seem to make sense.

After all, what did Julie know about college? In her mind it was nothing more than a daydream, a fuzzy series of movielike images: seminars and study groups, dorm parties and late-night bull sessions, football games and finals. But Matt's friendship, his love, the solid feeling of knowing he was there—all that was real. Now it was about to change. And Julie was scared.

"Hey, don't worry," Matt said. "You're gonna have a great time." His face was so close to hers that she could feel his breath on her cheek. Julie smiled. How did Matt always manage to know just what she was thinking? "You knew you wanted to go to Madison the second you got out there to visit, remember?"

Julie nodded. It was true; she'd been right at home at Madison College. Maybe it was the comfortable feeling of the small, close-knit college community. Or all the performances and events they held on campus. Or maybe just the good music that poured out of everyone's dorm room. The school had one of the best journalism programs in the country, too. Still, Julie wished she hadn't chosen a college that was so far away. Madison, Ohio. Right now it felt like the moon. "Write me?" Julie asked.

4

"Definitely." Matt's lips found the sensitive curve under her jaw. "I love this place right here," he said hoarsely. "And this one." He touched his mouth to her cheek, her temple, her closed eyes. Their mouths met again, and for a moment Julie was aware only of the way their bodies felt next to each other, the beat of her heart against his, the way his hands cradled her head and stroked her back. . . .

The blare of the car horn cut short the tenderness of their embrace. Julie darted a half-annoyed, half-embarrassed glance at her father in the driver's seat. She and Matt pulled slightly apart. "I guess this is it," Matt said. But he didn't let go of her.

Julie held him in her gaze. "Matt?"

"Yeah?"

"I love you," Julie whispered. She could feel her voice shaking.

"Me, too." Matt kissed her again. "Hey, I'll be waiting for you when you get back," he said. "Promise."

"Eleven weeks and three days till Thanksgiving vacation," Julie said. "And eight and a half hours," she added with a wink. Matt liked to tease her about how she always had all the facts.

He smiled. "You're gonna give 'em hell, Jules. Oops." He made a point of looking behind him to

5

where Julie's father sat in the car. "If the Reverend Miller will pardon my French. I mean heck."

Julie laughed—and blinked back her tears at the same time. "I'm gonna try," she said.

Matt wiped the beginnings of her tears away with the edge of his thumb, but his eyes were shiny, too. "Jules, it'll be good for you to go to a new place, go somewhere without any memories . . ."

Julie felt her chest tighten up. She squeezed her eyes shut and tried to push his words away. She didn't want to think about Mary Beth just then. It was a sad enough moment already. "I'll be fine," she said stiffly, blotting out the wrenching thoughts of her sister's death.

"Hey," Matt said gently, kissing the top of her head, "I know you will."

"Anyway, Matt, lots of my memories involve you—and I don't want to leave any of those behind," Julie said. She couldn't imagine how she was going to let go of him, walk across her front lawn past her cozy yellow house, and let her father drive her away.

"Well, we're going to make lots more memories, right?" Matt said. Julie wasn't sure if he was trying to reassure her, or if he wanted her to reassure him.

"Lots more," she said, making herself sound

steadier than she felt. She reached up and drew him to her in a final kiss. The horn sounded almost immediately. "Okay, okay," Julie mumbled under her breath. She took a step away from Matt but kept hold of him, sliding her palms down the length of his arms so that they were clasping hands.

"Bye," Matt said again.

"Bye," Julie repeated. They let go of each other.

"Just get out of here, okay?" Matt said lightly. He gave her a mock push on the shoulder.

Julie allowed herself one last look. Then she turned away and walked toward the car. She didn't glance back. Otherwise, she'd never be able to leave.

Now what? Matt wondered. He watched the Millers' station wagon, weighted down by all of Julie's stuff, disappear down Auger Street. It looked as if she were taking her whole life with her. Which sort of cut him out of the picture.

Matt felt a sting of doubt about his own choice. College was supposed to be the next step, wasn't it? You graduated from high school and you went to college. Then you graduated from college and got a job.

But Matt already had a job—one that he liked.

7

How many other people got to book their favorite bands and play host at Philly's best nightly party? And pretty soon his dad was going to promote him to manager of the Fast Lane. The club was named after his father's first career as a champion race car driver, and it was one of the hottest spots in Philadelphia. Good reason to stay put.

Besides, Matt had never been the biggest fan of school. He'd gotten decent marks, but he'd never gotten excited enough to really work at it. Sure, he liked to read, but what he wanted and when he wanted. And now he could do just that. Matt wasn't one to take the next step just because everyone else said it was the thing to do. Lots of other people followed the crowd and didn't seem any happier for it.

Still, it wasn't any fun to see so many of his friends splitting on him. Especially not Julie—his *best* friend. Matt let out a breath. He had a whole day without her before he had to be at work. No point in going home. His dad was probably still snoring away with Suzanna, his flavor of the month. And no way he could count on his mom. She said to call whenever he needed her, but it was just talk. As soon as the divorce from his dad had gone through, she'd picked up and moved to California. Now she was busy with her new family out there. Besides, it was six in the morning in San Francisco.

But, yo, buddy, don't go feeling sorry for yourself, Matt thought. He'd wanted to stay in Philly, and here he was. Maybe if his friend Steven wasn't busy, he'd be up for a little adventure. Good thing Steven had enrolled in the local community college and was sticking around. Maybe they could go for a hike—cruise to the Poconos for the afternoon, get some mountain air. Or at least take a trek through Fairmount Park. It was a good day for it. The heat wave had broken but it was still nice and sunny.

Matt started toward his shiny blue Harley, parked next to the curb in front of the house. The first thing to do was to get off the Millers' property. With Julie gone, it was now enemy turf. Reverend and Mrs. Miller didn't work too hard at disguising how they felt about him.

Matt swung one blue-jeaned leg over his motorcycle. Sometimes he felt as if he and Julie were Philadelphia's modern Romeo and Juliet. Would Julie's parents and his father ever stop feuding and declare peace? The Millers blamed Jerry Collins, Matt's dad, for the death of their older daughter, Mary Beth, two years back. The night of her fatal car crash, Mary Beth and her friends had been drinking at the Fast Lane—even

9

though they were underage. Mr. Collins blamed the Millers for the loss of business at the club after the accident. Was he responsible for Mary Beth's fake ID card? Was he responsible for her drinking and driving? Her father might be a reverend, but their daughter was no saint, Matt remembered him yelling not long after the accident.

At first, Matt couldn't have cared less what his father and the Millers said about each other. He was too bruised inside from his own grief. Mary Beth wasn't the only one who had lost her life that night. Mark Esposito, Mary Beth's boyfriend and Matt's best friend, had been a passenger in that car.

Matt fastened his motorcycle helmet securely as he remembered the wreck of Mary Beth's car, crumpled around a thick tree at the side of the road that ran past the Fast Lane. Mark and Mary Beth hadn't gotten very far after their night of partying at the club. Matt and Traci Clark, the girl he'd been seeing at the time, had downed a final beer with them and said good-bye. Matt had clapped Mark on the back and watched him leave the club holding hands with Mary Beth. Then Matt had helped Traci find her coat and walked her outside to her car. Their good-night kisses in the parking lot were getting pretty hot and heavy when the squeal of tires split the night. A beat later there was a sickening crash—the sound of crunching metal and shattering glass. And then a terrifying silence.

Matt had raced toward the accident, Traci right behind him. The rest of it had been a blur of nightmarish images—Traci's bloodcurdling scream, his own scream frozen in his throat, the bodies slumped forward in the wreck. He never clearly remembered going for help—his own beery haze was scrambled with his terror and shock. But then there had been the sirens—the ambulances, the police cars, their lights throwing a gruesome strobe on the trees along the road.

Matt had stood staring, mute. He'd felt helpless, sick, empty. For weeks afterward, he'd been tortured by the thought that there was nothing he could do. It couldn't be true. Mark and Mary Beth couldn't be gone forever. But they were.

After the accident, Matt had made himself a promise to stop drinking. He'd paid a condolence call on Mark's family and then on Mary Beth's, even though they were feuding with his father. The Millers hadn't made it easy. But he and Julie and Tommy had wound up sitting out in the backyard, telling funny stories about Mary Beth and Mark. Matt and Julie knew each other, but they'd never really sat down and talked before. Even

11

then, he'd thought she was really pretty, her thick brown hair framing a round face with strong features. He'd liked her broad smile, even though it was bittersweet with memories of her sister. But what he'd noticed most was the way her large brown eyes studied everything so intently—studied and understood.

When Tommy wandered back inside, Matt had found himself telling Julie how frustrated he felt that he couldn't somehow turn back the clock and stop Mary Beth and Mark from going out the club door. He'd played the scene out in his mind over and over, each time finding a different way of heading off the disaster.

"Yeah, I do that, too," Julie had said. "It's like these movies in my head, where everything happens differently than it really did." She'd made that motion with her head—the one where she tilted it to the side and looked as if she was listening to her own thoughts. "And then there's the movie where I at least get to say good-bye to her and tell her I love her." Her voice was wobbly. Then she was quiet for a long time, and when she'd spoken again, she was composed. "You know, I was so busy being the good little sister to her big, bad one, trying to do everything right when she did things wrong. She was pretty wild. I guess I don't have to tell you that." Matt remembered how Julie had given a soft, abbreviated laugh. "I never got to tell her how much I secretly admired her for it," she'd gone on. "I guess I was pretty jealous of the way she could let loose, no matter what Mom or Dad or anyone else said." Then Julie had smiled—the first real smile of Matt's visit. "I never admitted that to anyone before," she had said.

"I know how you feel," Matt had replied. "You want to do something, to say something to them. It's the most important thing in the whole world. But it's too late."

A few days later, in school, Julie had come up to Matt in the hall. "I have an idea," she said. "We could do something at the Fast Lane for everyone who knew my sister and Mark."

"You mean like a memorial of some kind?" Matt had asked doubtfully. In the wake of the accident, there was even talk of shutting the Fast Lane down.

"Well, maybe," Julie had said. "But a fun one. One that they'd approve of."

Matt and Julie had met after school, and together they'd thought up the idea of an alcohol-free, under-twenty-one night at the Fast Lane, complete with live music and lots of dancing. None for the Road Night, they called it. Matt had put all his steam into making it a weekly event at

13

the club. It wasn't the biggest night for making money, but it had brought back the community support for his father's business. And more important, it had brought Matt and Julie together.

It hadn't happened all at once. But little by little, Matt had stopped spending so much time with Traci and that crowd. That was when he'd first started realizing that following the crowd wasn't always the thing to do. Look where it had gotten Mark and Mary Beth. All of their old pals had pretty much drifted apart since the crash. It wasn't like they weren't friendly, but it wasn't the same as before. Out of the old crowd, Matt had stayed close only to Steven—and the accident had sobered Steven up pretty fast, too.

Meanwhile, Matt had found himself spending more and more time with Julie. First it was because they were planning None for the Road Night. Or swapping memories of Mary Beth or Mark, sometimes hugging away each other's tears. But they made each other laugh, too. They had fun together. Matt had taught Julie how to cross-country ski. Julie had read him her favorite poems. They'd become real friends. And then more than friends.

Matt turned his key in the ignition and revved up his bike. It made a comfortingly loud purr. He patted the gas tank of his bike, took one last look at Julie's two-floor, lemon-yellow house, and roared down the street toward Steven's.

Their parents might not agree, but Matt and Julie were a great couple. He hated to think about what it was going to be like in Philly without her.

Two

❧

Julie's half of the divided double dorm room
could barely hold her entire family. Tommy sat
on an upended suitcase by the window, and her
parents stood stiffly in the middle of all the boxes
and bags. Julie sat on the edge of her bed, not
quite believing that this was her new home. Her
little half of Wilson Hall room 103, the inside half,
had a simple pine desk, a set of bookshelves, a
telephone, an overhead fluorescent light fixture,
and a full-length mirror on the back of the door
that led to the outside half of the room. Without
any decorations, it looked an awful lot like a room
in a cheap motel chain—an anonymous room that
wasn't a home to anyone. Julie was going to have
to do something about that, and fast.

Her roommate's side wasn't too different. It

16

had its own desk and bookshelves, and it also had a built-in dresser and closet for both of them.

Julie couldn't wait to meet her new roommate. So far, all she knew was her name and where she was from. Dahlia Sussman from New York City. That was what the housing card said. The idea of living with a complete stranger for a whole year was pretty bizarre. "I wonder when my roommate'll get here," Julie said to no one in particular.

Tommy leaned out the open window. "Maybe that's her, getting out of that car in front of the dorm," he said. Julie felt a tremor of anticipation. She started to get up.

"Nope," Tommy amended. "Ohio license plate. Besides, she doesn't look like she's from New York City."

Julie laughed as she sank back down. "Tommy, what do you think someone from New York looks like, anyway?"

Tommy gave an embarrassed shrug. "I don't know. Sort of stylish and stuff—like those girls in magazines."

"Tommy, not everyone from New York is a fashion plate, you know," Julie said.

"Well, too bad we're not going to get to meet her," Reverend Miller said. "I'd like to wait a while longer and see if she arrives, but it's a long trip back."

"That's okay, Dad," Julie said. "I'll write you all about her."

College and parents just didn't seem to go together, and the truth was that Julie wanted to be on her own. Her folks and Tommy had stayed at the Madison Inn the night before, but bright and early—too early—they'd knocked on her door, and they'd all gone out to breakfast at the Black Angus Coffee Shop. So far it had been like a weird kind of family vacation. Now that she was at Madison, Julie was eager for her real college life to begin.

But saying good-bye was another story. No one mentioned it out loud, but Julie knew they were all thinking about Mary Beth. Her parents' somber expressions told her how hard it was for them to be saying good-bye to their other daughter. Julie wished she could do something to smooth away their sad faces, but deep down she also felt a stirring of relief. Ever since the accident, she'd felt that somehow she had to be two times the daughter to them, covering for the emptiness they all suffered. Maybe one of the best things about college would be getting away from all of that.

18

"I know you'll make us proud," her father said formally, confirming what Julie was thinking.

Julie nodded. Of course she would. Didn't she always?

"It's going to be a wonderful semester," her mother put in, coming over to rest a tentative hand on Julie's shoulder. "New experiences, new people." Her voice emphasized the "new people."

Julie stiffened under her mother's touch. She knew what her mother was really trying to say. She didn't mean new people; she meant new boys. Better boys. Boys who were more like Julie. Wouldn't her parents love it if she met someone who'd take Matt's place? Well, that wasn't going to happen.

"Well . . ." Her father shifted from one foot to the other. "I suppose we'd better get going."

"I suppose so," her mother echoed, her hand still on Julie's shoulder.

Julie stood up, her face level with her mother's. People said they looked alike—the same large brown eyes, round face, broad mouth, ever-so-slight upward tilt of the nose. But her mother's face was set; there were tiny, unyielding lines around her mouth, as if she had determined to hold her ground no matter what life threw her way. There was a brief, frozen moment, as if they were both considering what to do. Then they simultaneously wrapped their arms around each other in a big hug.

"Mom, I promise to write once a week and eat all my vegetables," Julie joked, giving her mother a big kiss.

Her father gave her a big hug, too. "I can't believe my baby's a college girl," he said in a rare show of tenderness.

Julie hugged Tommy the hardest, even though he pretended to hate it. It was going to be tough on him now that he was the only child left at home. "Keep an eye on Matt," she told him. "Don't let him get into too much trouble. And you either, okay, sport?" She gave him a loud smack of a kiss on the cheek.

"Gross, Julie," he said.

"See you at Thanksgiving, sweetheart," her mother said.

"Call us when you're all settled in," her father said.

"I will," Julie said. "Have a good trip back." There was another round of hugs. Julie walked them out into the hall. Her mother and Tommy both turned and waved just before they got to the exit. Then Julie was alone. Really alone.

She went back inside and flopped down on her bed, staring at all her boxes and bags. She knew she ought to unpack, but she just didn't feel like it. *Somehow*, she thought, *my first day of college ought to start off with something a little more interesting.*

If Matt were there, he'd probably come up with some adventure right away. Julie wondered what he was doing at that moment. Sleeping, probably, after a night of work at the Fast Lane. She wished she could wake him up with soft kisses on his closed eyelids. Julie sighed. It still felt like the hugest mistake of her life to have left Matt hundreds of miles away.

She got up and wandered over to the window. Across the road from the dorm were acres of brown fields, marked by the dried, withered stalks of the summer's corn crop. The landscape stretched out flat for as far as the eye could see, crowned by a huge blue sky. *A person could feel lost out here*, Julie thought. *Totally lost.*

She turned away from the window and frowned at her still-packed suitcases. Maybe she'd go explore the town and unpack later. She found her sneakers half hidden in the mess on her floor. As she put them on she looked through the open door to the other half of the room. Dahlia's half. Julie wished her roommate would hurry up and get there. Was Dahlia on a plane at that moment? Or in a car with her parents, feeling nervous about starting college? Was she a little

21

homesick already? Maybe she had just said good-bye to some special boy.

Julie stood up and walked through the outer room. She hoped that when she got back she'd find out.

Dahlia barely waited until Paul had shut the passenger door. She slammed her foot down on the accelerator and peeled away from the curb. "Let's blow this town!" she yelled. She felt her long hair streaming out behind her as her BMW picked up speed. She loved driving this car. It was so smooth and fast. "Good-bye, one o'clock curfew, good-bye, school uniforms, good-bye, Mom and Dad!"

"Excellent!" Paul said. "Party on!"

Dahlia gave him a sidelong glance and shook her head ever so slightly. Paul Chase was hopeless. In those cutoff jeans with the strings hanging down his thighs, his long curly hair, that black T-shirt with the sleeves hacked off, and the peace-sign medallion he wore around his neck, he looked like a cross between a metalhead and a flower child. Paul could be really fun sometimes. They'd been friends practically forever. But Dahlia was not psyched to have her past follow her out to college. Definitely not psyched.

"Hey, you want to put something on the

stereo?" Dahlia asked, trying not to sound too irritated with Paul. In a way, it was sweet that he was still so crazy about her. "There's a bunch of CDs in the glove compartment."

"I've got some, too," Paul said, reaching for the knapsack on the floor at his feet.

Dahlia sped through a yellow light and slammed on her brakes at the next red one. "Okay, but we're not listening to your party mix for the next eight hours," she said. "Reminds me too much of high school." She watched two men in running clothes jog across the street toward Central Park. A woman passed in front of her car carrying a blue-and-white shopping bag from Sussman's department store. Dahlia was used to seeing the family logo all over town. She was looking forward to getting away from it for a while.

"How about some Dorothy's Dilemma?" Paul asked. "They're my friend's band. I've got their demo."

"How about not," Dahlia said. She handed him a CD and pulled away from the light. "Here, put this in. And crank it!" She loved a road trip. Loud music, new things to see, weird truck stops in the middle of nowhere. Paul wasn't exactly new scenery, but Dahlia was in such a good mood that she didn't care. "I'm so psyched!" she said, racing past the tall buildings of New York's ritzy Upper East Side, guarded by a battalion of uniformed doormen.

"Yeah, me, too," Paul said, turning up the volume. "But there's some stuff I'll miss. Frisbee in the park, all the concerts, the clubs . . ."

"The clubs!" Dahlia added over the first notes of music. "And of course shopping. But here's to wild times at college!"

"Killer!" Paul said. Paul's lingo could get annoying, Dahlia thought, except that nothing was going to spoil her day. A really cute guy with dark skin and dark hair and a cool pair of shades crossed the street at the next light, glancing over at her sporty red car. Dahlia grinned at him. *Oh well, there are hot guys everywhere,* she figured.

"So," Paul said a few minutes later, "aren't you gonna miss what's-his-name?"

"Who?" Dahlia asked.

"That guy I heard you spent a lot of time with out in the Hamptons this summer." He drummed his fingers on the dashboard in time to the music.

"Oh, him," Dahlia said. Sometimes New York seemed like a tiny town, the way word got around. She thought about her last night with Jason, skinny-dipping on the East Hampton beach, with the stars clear and crisp and the sound of the waves pounding against the sand. It had definitely been fun. But she was sure she was going to have plenty more fun when she got out to Madison. "It was just an S.R.—summer romance. You know, fun in the sun," she said. "This is one woman who's starting off her college career totally unattached!" she added pointedly. She didn't want Paul to get any ideas just because she was letting him bum a ride out to school.

"Oh," Paul said. After a pause he added, "Don't you think it's pretty cosmic, you know, the two of us going to the same college and stuff? After knowing each other practically forever?"

Dahlia gave a noncommittal shrug.

"I think it's intense," Paul went on.

Dahlia steered the car onto the highway along the East River. The towers of steel and brick sped by against the sky. Soon they'd be far away. "Like I said, Chase, freedom. I'm free as a bird. Watch out, Madison College!"

Three

❧

Whoa! Julie thought. *Tommy was right. She does look like she's straight out of a fashion magazine.* Julie had just finished unpacking her final suitcase when she heard the door opening. In breezed a tall, striking girl with long, streaked blond hair, a suntan, and a pleated black skirt that was as short as her legs were long. A cropped black tank top, a pair of black lizard-skin cowboy booties—no socks—and a pair of dangly, gem-studded earrings completed the outfit.

Julie felt instantly unchic in her khaki shorts and the Madison College T-shirt she'd bought in town earlier—purple and white with the words "I'm a Madison Madwoman" on it. "Dahlia?" Julie said tentatively, even though she knew that's who it was.

"Julie! Hey!" Dahlia said, as if they knew each

26

other already. She dropped her leather drawstring-topped bag in the middle of the floor, glanced around the room, and then poked her head into Julie's half of the room. "Oh, you beat me to the inside room, huh?" she asked lightly. "Well, I guess we can switch for the second semester, right?"

Julie felt a little taken aback. Dahlia certainly said what was on her mind. Julie wasn't sure if that was good or bad. "Well, sure," she said, wondering if she should have waited before she'd made herself at home in the inside room. But if Dahlia had gotten there first, wouldn't she have done the same? Julie was sure she would have.

Dahlia went over to her bed and tested the mattress with her hand. "Home sweet home."

Julie laughed a little nervously. There was a momentary lull. They looked at each other and smiled. No question about it. The girl wasn't just pretty; she was gorgeous. "So, um, how was your trip from New York?" Julie asked politely. "How'd you get out here?" She noticed that Dahlia's parents were nowhere in sight.

"Drove my car," Dahlia said.

"You've got a car?" Julie asked, immediately feeling a little stupid for stating the obvious.

Dahlia laughed. "Yeah. It's parked in the lot out back."

"Wow!" Julie said. "A roommate with wheels, huh?"

"You got it, roomie. The wheel is woman's greatest invention! I wouldn't go anywhere without them."

Julie laughed again, feeling a little less shy. Dahlia had her own kind of energy, that was for sure. Julie was fairly certain she was going to like it. "So . . . did you drive out here all by yourself?" It was an awfully long trip from New York —at least as long as from Philadelphia.

Dahlia shook her head, her earrings bobbing and her hair swirling. "Nah. This guy—I know him from high school and he's starting here, too —he drove out with me."

"Neat!" Julie said, instantly thinking that she sounded like a girl scout on a picnic. Her new roommate probably never used words like *neat*.

"It was all right," Dahlia said. "Same as always with Paul. He drooled over me for eight hours. Seemed like eight days. I mean, don't get me wrong. He's an okay guy and all, but after eight hours in the car with him it was a relief to dump him at his dorm."

"Oh." Julie sure hoped Dahlia wouldn't get tired of her that quickly. After all, they were going to be stuck together for a whole year. "Well, you must be exhausted after the long trip," she said. "You wanna take a nap or something?"

Dahlia tossed her head. "Nap? During my first hour of college? No way!" She went over to her bag and got out a hairbrush. "I feel sort of like a mess, though, after the drive," she said, her eyes darting around the walls of her room.

"Mirror?" Julie asked. "It's on my side. The phone, too."

"No way!" Dahlia opened her blue eyes wide, the hairbrush clutched in her hand. "Who designed this place?"

"Well, you've got the chest of drawers and the closet," Julie assured her. "I put my stuff away—but I saved you more than half the space," she added quickly. "Where's your stuff, anyway? Want me to help you get it from the car?"

Dahlia let out a loud gasp. She spun around, her gaze traveling to all corners of the room. "Oh, my God!" she exclaimed. "My stuff! Where is it? Didn't it get here?"

"What do you mean?" Julie asked. "Didn't you bring it out with you?"

"In my little convertible? No way it could fit," Dahlia said, her voice edged with panic. "I sent it out two weeks ago. It should have been delivered right to the room!"

Julie raised her shoulders and let them drop.

29

Dahlia tossed her hairbrush onto her bed. "I've gotta call home." She raced into Julie's half of the room, grabbed the telephone receiver, and began punching buttons. Julie watched her pace impatiently. Then she looked at Julie and rolled her eyes. "Answering machine," she said. "Hi, Daddy? My stuff's not here, and I don't even have a change of clothes! Call me as soon as possible, okay? Bye." She recited the phone number, then hung up and plunked down on Julie's bed. "Oh, man! Major drag," she said.

"Really," Julie agreed. "But listen, you're welcome to borrow some of my clothes."

She felt Dahlia giving her T-shirt and shorts the once-over. "Hey, that's really sweet of you," Dahlia said. "But you know what?" She let out a big, noisy breath. "I'm not going to get all freaked out about this."

Julie laughed. "You're not?"

Dahlia laughed, too. "No. Forget the last three minutes, okay? I think my stuff not getting here is a sign. Yeah, I think this means we're supposed to go on a shopping trip," Dahlia said happily.

"Here? Now? It's almost five o'clock," Julie said. "The stores'll be closing soon, and there's this freshman orientation picnic later."

Dahlia stood up. "We'd better hurry."

30

Julie laughed. One thing was for sure: life wasn't going to be dull around room 103.

Matt stood barefoot in his kitchen and dialed the Ohio area code and Julie's new phone number. They'd agreed to keep it to a call a week and write instead, but Matt wanted to make sure Julie had gotten there okay. At least that was his excuse. Truth was, he needed to hear her voice.

Instead, it was Steven's voice that played in his mind. "You've gotta quit moping, man," he'd said as they sat by a stream in the woods the day before, their trail bikes next to them on the ground. "You're free! Enjoy it, dude!"

But all Matt felt was empty. At work, he couldn't stop looking at the clock, couldn't get into the music even though it was a hot new band he'd been really psyched about booking. He could barely manage to keep the drink orders straight. He'd really thought he knew what he wanted when he'd decided to stay in Philadelphia and work at the Fast Lane. Now he was afraid it would be just the same old routine, night after night. It had been only one lonely day, but Matt had a feeling there were going to be plenty more like it.

Julie's phone rang. Matt waited, pulling the phone over to the refrigerator and looking inside to see what he could find. It rang some more. A plastic container of leftover spaghetti, a couple of overripe bananas . . . Matt let the phone ring a few more times. He shut the refrigerator and hung up. He wasn't hungry, anyway. Just bored. Where was Julie? What was she doing? What was it like out there in Ohio?

The idea of college conjured up images of stately stone buildings, green lawns, students walking with their arms full of books, a mammoth and busy library, people hanging out on the grass in little groups. Matt tried to imagine Julie in each of those places, but he couldn't get a fix on the picture. It was unreal, not connected to anything he knew, as if he were mentally taking a cutout of Julie and pasting it against the photos in a catalog for Any College, U.S.A.

Now, picturing her in Philadelphia—that was another thing. He had no problem envisioning Julie by the stream where he'd gone with Steven the day before. In fact, it hadn't been very long since he'd been there with her. They'd packed a picnic lunch and spread a blanket out on a patch of ground where the sun splashed through the tree branches in lacy, gently shifting patterns. They'd taken off their shoes and waded in the icy, rushing water, and after lunch they'd stretched out on the blanket and made up stories

32

about where the stream started and all the places it ran through before and after passing that spot. Their spot, they'd called it. They'd ended up lying on the blanket kissing to the sound of the stream flowing over the rocks. Matt sat down at the kitchen table. He knew he had a dopey grin on his face.

"Hi there, Matt!" sang out a teasing voice with a faint Southern lilt.

"Oh, Suzanna. Hi." She had on the skimpiest pair of shorts imaginable and a man's V-neck T-shirt. With her short blond hair and her petite, curvy body, she looked great, but she hardly fit the part of a father's girlfriend. *Except if you know my father,* Matt thought.

"And what's our handsome, eligible bachelor up to today?" Suzanna asked, filling the kettle with water. "Want a cup of coffee?"

Matt shook his head. His memory of the picnic with Julie was gone, and so was his dopey smile.

"Hey, don't look so bent out of shape, sweetie," Suzanna said. "You'll get over her. There are plenty of other pebbles on the beach."

Matt gave a short, hard laugh. "Julie's not your average pebble," he said, trying to make a joke out of it but sounding pretty miserable.

Suzanna took his hand and gave it a little squeeze. "You got it bad, huh, sweetie?"

Matt nodded. "Yeah, I guess I do." Bad, good —with Julie so far away, Matt wasn't sure which it was.

Julie turned her face up to catch the wind as Dahlia sped the little convertible toward town, braking only for the briefest fraction of a second at the stop sign on Main Street.

"Left here," Julie instructed. "These two blocks have most of the stores."

Dahlia pulled around the corner with a screech of rubber. "Two blocks? That's it? I mean, this is it?"

"Like I said, Dahlia," Julie laughed, "we really didn't have to drive. Although your car is amazingly cool. Matt would love it."

Dahlia slowed down and cruised past the Black Angus Coffee Shop and Books and Things, where Julie had bought her Madison T-shirt. "Flower shop, bakery, barbershop, complete with one of those candy-cane poles," Dahlia reeled off as they drove by. "Hey, check it out, a drugstore with a soda fountain. A fifty-nine-cent shop? Unbelievable. This place is a trip. It's like a time capsule or something."

"Yeah, it's pretty sweet, isn't it?" Julie said.

"The soda fountain's even got one of those long counters with the high, round swivel stools built into the floor, like you see in old movies. Dreamy, in a way."

"Sweet? Dreamy? Yeah, I guess," Dahlia said with a chuckle. "But it's gonna be something, spending four years of my life out in the boonies like this." She pulled the car over to the curb and turned off the engine. "Well, at least there's no parking problem here. Okay, Julie, you win. We can walk from here."

Julie laughed as she got out of the car. "Dahlia, didn't you come out for a visit and an interview when you were deciding on colleges?"

Dahlia shook her head. "Nah. Madison's my dad's alma mater, so it was kind of decided for me. To tell you the truth, it was fine with me because it was the farthest place from home that I applied to." She shut her door and dropped the keys in her bag.

A couple of men in navy work pants and caps walked by. One of them had a tool belt slung around his hips. They both gave a hard look at the red sports car, and at Julie and Dahlia. Especially at Dahlia. It wasn't a friendly look. Julie felt as if she and Dahlia were wearing signs: Rich College Kids.

"Jeez," Dahlia said in a low voice, grabbing Julie's arm and steering her in the opposite direction. "Haven't they ever seen city people before?"

Julie shrugged. "I guess that's the problem. They've probably seen too many of us. I think we've invaded their turf."

They walked past the Madison Volunteer Fire Department. The firehouse door was open, and inside were two small but gleaming red fire trucks. "Well, I hope some people are a little friendlier," Dahlia said.

"They are," Julie assured her. "The people in the bookstore were really nice to me—wanted to know where I was from and everything. They said they'd been in Philly a few years ago and visited the Liberty Bell. Oh, here's the dress shop." She stopped in front of a little store with one big glass window. One mannequin had on a dark red pants suit; the other wore a tailored blue skirt and a silky blouse that tied in a bow at the neck. Not exactly the latest fashion from Paris.

"Frump city," Dahlia groaned. "Looks like they haven't changed their window display since the Polyester Era."

"Yeah, I didn't think you were going to be too excited about it," Julie said. "but there's a thrift store around the corner. I went in earlier. There's this really beautiful beaded dress I tried on."

Dahlia gave Julie an impulsive hug. "Good

work, Julie! Thrift shops are my favorite," she said. "I knew there was some reason the housing office put us together."

A few minutes later, Julie was, for the second time that day, trying on the cream-colored sleeveless dress embroidered with an intricate pattern of pearllike beads. She looked in the mirror of the dressing room. The dress hugged her body, but not too tightly, tapering at the bottom and ending a little above the knee. The light, shimmery fabric set off her dark hair and eyes.

"It looks fabulous," Dahlia said when Julie stepped out from behind the dressing room curtain. In the few minutes it had taken Julie to change, Dahlia had already managed to pick through several racks. A hefty pile of clothes was draped over her arm.

Julie smoothed her hands over her hips. "I shouldn't be doing this," she told Dahlia. "I almost couldn't resist buying it the first time."

"Well, then it's a good thing I got you back in here," Dahlia said matter-of-factly. She held a silver metallic knit dress up to herself. "Is this too much?"

"Well, it's a little . . ."

"Tacky? Well, tacky's fun sometimes. I think I'll try it on. Now, about that dress—you're gonna buy it, right?"

Julie shook her head. "I love it, but it's fifty dollars."

"Fifty? Oh, my God! Total bargain," Dahlia said. "That dress would cost at least a hundred in New York."

Julie sighed. "Dahlia, the school's giving me a job at one of the dining halls, but it hasn't started yet. Besides, I think they expect me to spend the money on books and laundry and stuff."

But the girl just didn't take no for an answer. "Wait till Pat sees you in it." Dahlia added a few more items to her try-on pile.

"Matt," Julie said. "And as long as I'm out here and he's in Philadelphia, he's *not* going to see me in it." That pretty much decided it for her. "Here, can you unzip me?"

"Look, how about this?" Dahlia said. "I'll try the dress on, too. If it looks okay on me, I'm buying us a housewarming present."

"Oh, come on, Dahlia. I can live without it." Julie knew Dahlia was doing it for her.

"Forget it," Dahlia said. "It's settled."

"Dahlia, you just met me."

"Julie, I live with you."

Of course the dress looked great on Dahlia. And of course they left Secondhand Rose with it —and two other bags of clothes as well.

Four

Julie's new next-door neighbor, Marion, sighed. "Boys and food," she said with total sincerity. "I think college is going to be wonderful."

Julie laughed. She was sitting cross-legged on the campus's North Quad with a paper plate heaped with cold cuts, potato salad, macaroni salad, and coleslaw balanced on her knee. The quad, a large, lush rectangle of grass bordered by a half-dozen modern brick dormitories, was teeming with freshmen enjoying the orientation picnic. "I read that college girls gain an average of ten pounds during their freshman year," Julie said.

"You don't look like you have to worry," said Sarah, one of the girls from the triple at the end of Julie's hall. Sarah was from Colorado, and she had an older brother who was a Madman, too.

"Anyway, you've got a boyfriend back home, right?" Marion said longingly. "I bet he's cute, too."

Julie nodded, blushing a little. "Adorable."

"Lucky you," Marion said. "I mean, not that I think that just because you have a boyfriend already you should turn into the Goodyear blimp," she added quickly.

Julie and Sarah cracked up. Julie had a feeling that Marion didn't have any idea how funny she was. Marion's roommate, Susan, put a hand over her mouth and giggled quietly. Susan was a violinist studying at the Madison Music Conservatory, and Marion had been proud to announce that her roommate had given concerts all over the world. Julie found it hard to picture Susan standing up in front of hundreds of people and playing with confidence. Offstage she was so shy.

"Hi. Mind if we sit down?" asked a very tall, pretty black girl, coming over with a plate of food. At her side was a chunky, freckle-faced girl with red curls.

"Hi, guys," Sarah said. "Everybody, these are my two roommates, Gwendolyn and Amanda. And this is Julie and Marion and Susan."

"Hi," everyone said, more or less in unison.

"We were just getting into my two favorite subjects—boys and food," Sarah said.

"You mean we were getting into our food," Marion said. "The boys, well . . . we were only talking about them."

"Except Julie's roommate," Sarah said, pointing out Dahlia, who was over by the long table of food and beverages, talking to a lean, muscular boy with wavy blond hair.

"That's Andy from upstairs," Julie said. He and Dahlia were leaning in close to each other, laughing as if they had some private joke. Behind Dahlia, sipping at whatever was in his cup and trying to look casual, was that skinny, curly-haired friend of hers from home, Paul Chase. Dahlia had introduced him to Julie at the beginning of the picnic and then quickly left them to make conversation on their own. Paul was a little flaky but smart. He and Julie had talked about their favorite books for a while, and then Paul had said something about getting another drink—and gone off to hunt for Dahlia, Julie was sure. The poor guy was totally smitten.

Marion was looking at Dahlia and sighing again. "Maybe that'll be me one day soon," she said dreamily.

Somehow, Julie couldn't see round, apple-cheeked Marion in Dahlia's all-black New York outfit, flirting and laughing with a guy like Andy. Marion had told Julie that she was from a farm not too far from school—and in her baggy shorts and short-sleeved button-down shirt, her brown hair in two braids, she certainly looked it. She must have been the one Dahlia was talking about when she'd told Julie she thought there was someone on their hall from Kansas. Julie held in a laugh. What was it about New Yorkers and geography? If it weren't for *The Wizard of Oz,* they probably wouldn't know a single thing about any place between the East Coast and the Rocky Mountains. *I don't think we're in Manhattan anymore, Toto.*

"I can't even imagine being able to talk to a guy like that," Marion was saying, pushing her fork around her plate as if just thinking about talking to a boy made her nervous.

"Why not?" Gwendolyn asked. "Boys are people. Sort of."

They all laughed—even Susan, who hadn't said anything since they'd arrived at the picnic.

"What about you, Susan?" Julie said, trying to draw her into the conversation. "Do you have a boyfriend back home?"

Susan lowered her eyes to the ground. "Well, there's one boy, but . . . I don't know him very well."

"Yeah," Marion commiserated. "I've got someone like that at home. A couple of them, actually."

Susan gave a soft laugh. "No, it's not like that," she said. "See, he's the son of my father's business partner back in Korea. Our parents have decided that we should be together."

"Wow, you mean like an arranged marriage?" Amanda exclaimed.

"Maybe." Susan looked embarrassed. "I've tried to tell my parents that it's different for me, growing up here, than it was for them, but . . ."

"And *I* thought *I* had problems because my parents don't like my boyfriend!" Julie said.

"I can't imagine being married to *anyone*," Sarah said.

"Yeah. Like, let me start with a boyfriend," Marion added.

"I don't know," Julie mused, remembering the feel of Matt's lips when she'd kissed him good-bye on her front lawn. "I think maybe someday I could see getting married to Matt . . . if we get through the next four years," she added. She looked around the quad and tried to picture Matt milling around with a plate of food, talking about where he was from, what classes he was going to sign up for, and who his roommate was.

But what was the point? She knew that at this time of the evening, Matt would just be starting his shift at the Fast Lane. At that moment he was probably putting away glasses and setting tables,

43

getting the club ready before it opened for the night. She could see him in his faded jeans and white T-shirt, his arm muscles defined as he wiped down the club's long, dark wood bar. The night's band would be up on the stage, setting up their instruments and doing a sound check. "Needs a little more bass from back here," Matt might be saying.

Julie put her half-finished plate of food down on the ground next to her and wrapped her arms around her knees, pulling them in tight to her chest. She'd had a great time in town with Dahlia, and it was fun to be meeting all her new neighbors and classmates, but all this talk about boys was making her miss Matt, big-time. As soon as the picnic was over she was going to call him— once-a-week rule or not.

"Hello, Fast Lane," said Matt's familiar, slightly pebbly tenor.

Julie felt a huge smile stretching across her face. It was so good to hear Matt's voice. In the background, the band was warming up and people were laughing and talking at high volume. It was good to hear the sound of the club, too. "Hi, handsome."

"Jules!" Matt said happily. "Can you hear me?"

"Barely," Julie said. "But it's okay. It sounds like home."

"Huh?"

Julie laughed. "I said it sounds like home," she yelled into the receiver. "It's kind of nice."

"Man, it's kind of nice to hear you, too," Matt yelled back. "I tried to call you earlier, but no one was there. What've you been up to?"

Julie told him about her trip to town with Dahlia and the picnic and the kids on her hall. "Everyone's really nice. Really different. This one girl, Marion, she grew up on a farm and she's never been out of Ohio. And her roommate was born in Korea and she's lived in all these different places. I don't know how they got put together."

"And your roommate? This Dahlia person?" Matt asked, over the growing racket at the Fast Lane.

"I think I'm really going to like her," Julie said. "I don't exactly know where she is right now. The last I saw her, she was talking to this cute guy at the picnic."

On the other end, Matt was silent. The noise in the club seemed to swell through the telephone line. "Matt?" Julie said.

"Yeah, I'm here." Julie could hear the tightness that had crept into his voice. All of a sudden, she realized why.

"Oh, come on, Matt. *Dahlia's* with a guy—not me. Besides, you mean to tell me there aren't any pretty girls hanging out at the Fast Lane right now?" she said.

"Well . . . yeah," Matt said. "A few, I guess."

"And don't you still miss me like crazy?" Julie asked.

"Definitely," Matt said, more firmly.

Julie felt a flush of warmth. "Okay. I rest my case."

Matt laughed. "Have you switched from journalism to law already? Look, I'm sorry, Jules. I guess the thought of all those college Joes kind of bums me out," he admitted.

"Well, don't let it," Julie said. "I totally miss you. Now how about telling me exactly what you're doing and what you're wearing and everything about the past two days?" She settled down on her bed and kicked off her sneakers.

For the next twenty minutes, Julie almost forgot that Matt was four hundred miles away. Except that they found themselves talking louder and louder as the action in the Fast Lane heated up. "Yeah, the first band's about to come on," Matt told her. "Federal Deficit. They're pretty good."

46

Suddenly, Julie felt her chest constricting. "I wish I were with you," she said.

"Same here, Jules. Just a sec, Dad. I'm talking to Julie!" Matt screamed.

"Look, Matt, I know you're busy," Julie said reluctantly. "We'll talk real soon, right? I miss you, don't forget."

"And don't forget that I miss you, too, Jules. A lot."

There was a long, terrible pause. "Well . . ." Julie finally said.

"Well . . ." Matt echoed. Then he laughed.

"What?" Julie asked.

"I don't know. I don't suppose you'd want to bag school and run off with me and get married?" Matt joked.

Julie thought of the conversation she'd had on the quad with the girls from her hall. "Ask me in four years. I love you, Matt."

"I love you, too, Jules."

Julie waited until she heard the click on Matt's end. She let out a noisy sigh and hung up. Four years. Four years of phone calls. Four whole years. She was convinced that she'd marry Matt in four years—if they lasted that long. She stood and stared at the telephone for a long time. Matt was awfully far away.

* * *

As the band came out and the crowd in the Fast Lane surged toward the stage, Matt slumped down in a chair at the end of the bar, resting his chin in his hands. He felt miserable, and it was only day two without Julie.

"Well, someone's looking a little bummed out," said a high voice behind him. Matt turned as Traci settled down next to him, pulling her chair close to his. Her auburn hair was long and loose, and Matt could smell her perfume.

"Oh, hey, Traci. I didn't know you were here tonight."

"Yeah, I came with Tina. She's up in front making eyes at the drummer," Traci said over the first wail of guitar chords.

Matt gave a little laugh. "Figures. And what about you? Aren't you into Federal Deficit? I thought they were pretty hot when I booked them."

"Yeah, they're good," Traci said. "But I saw you back here looking like a sad little puppy, and I figured you could use some cheering up." She reached up and ruffled his hair.

"That obvious, huh?"

"Hey, I could always tell when things were getting you down," Traci said lightly. "Still can."

Matt made a feeble attempt at a smile. "Nah, I'm okay. Just . . . thinking."

"Yeah, I know—about how Ohio's a pretty long way away, huh?"

Matt broke into a real smile. "Okay, guilty as charged. I was thinking about Julie."

"It's tough," Traci said. "When Charlie left for the Marine Corps, I scarfed down a whole gallon of ice cream in one night."

"You heard from him lately?" Matt asked.

"Nope." Traci shook her head. "It's too hard trying to keep it together long-distance like that. I mean, he's signed up for three years, you know?"

Matt felt his mood dive even lower. "Yeah. I know," he said pointedly. "Three years, four years. What's the difference?"

"Oops." Traci slapped a hand over her mouth, her silver rings flashing. "I didn't mean it that way, Matt. I meant for me and Charlie."

Matt raised an eyebrow. "Well, it's gonna be different with me and Julie. I hope," he added a little uncertainly.

Traci slung an arm around his shoulder. Matt could feel the side of her body pressing against his. "Maybe it will be," she said. "I just don't like to see you looking so down."

"Thanks, Trace," Matt said. He knew she meant it. Even though he and Traci had grown apart, they'd never lost a certain warmth for each other, a kind of nostalgic nod to the times they'd once shared.

"The first few days are the worst," Traci said sympathetically.

"Yeah, she just left yesterday, and already I can't stand it," Matt said.

"It'll get easier." Traci tapped her foot to Federal Deficit's beat.

"Yeah? What about absence making the heart grow fonder?" Matt asked.

"What about out of sight, out of mind?" Traci tossed back.

Matt laughed. "Forget it, Traci."

"Made you laugh," she said. "Now how about a beer for an old friend?"

"Can't," Matt said. "And you know it. I only serve 'em. I can't drink 'em, and neither can you."

"I can't, but I do," Traci said.

Matt rolled his eyes. "Look, I didn't ask you how you got in here, or mention your fake ID card," he said. "How about we just leave it at that?"

Traci smiled easily. "Okay. If you dance with me instead." She stood up and took Matt's hand. Her tank top and jeans followed every curve.

Matt stayed put. "Traci, I'm pining away, remember?" he said lightly.

Traci tugged on his hand. "Matt, you're not

50

gonna love Julie any less if you let yourself have a little fun," she argued. "And I remember you used to be pretty good at having fun."

Matt stood up and laughed. "Why don't you just go away and let me be miserable?" he said as he followed her out to the dance floor.

Five

❦

"Okay, who's the cutest guy in here?" Dahlia whispered to Julie.

The large basement room was windowless, with harsh fluorescent lighting glaring down on the tables full of forms and course descriptions, the brusque, busy registrars behind the tables, and the endless lines of students waiting to sign up for classes. Not the most romantic spot in the galaxy.

Julie grinned anyway. "Dahlia, you're supposed to be choosing classes, not boyfriends," she whispered back, shuffling forward as the line moved up slowly. She had her fingers crossed that the journalism class she wanted to take wouldn't be full by the time they got to the front of the line. "Besides, what about Andy from upstairs?" That was one thing she had already learned at Madison, she thought with amusement. People in college didn't have last names. Instead, they were Andy from upstairs, Marion from the farm, Dahlia with the long blond hair.

"Andy's great," Dahlia said. "Total hunk. Did I tell you he's taking me to the Barn and Grill for dinner tonight? It's off campus—it's supposed to be real cool. They turned this old barn into a restaurant."

"Oh, yeah. Sarah from the triple was telling me about that place. Her brother and a lot of his buddies from the football team hang out there. She said they have a great jukebox."

"Good music, good food, and a gorgeous man —sounds like my kind of night," Dahlia said approvingly. "Maybe I'll wear my new silver dress. Daddy said they're looking for my boxes, but until they show up, I'm gonna have to make do with the stuff I got from the thrift shop." She shrugged. "I don't know. Maybe silver's too tony for a barn."

"You could wear the beaded dress," Julie suggested. "Don't forget it's half yours."

"Looks better on you," Dahlia said. Julie doubted it. Dahlia had a way of turning even the most basic, boring T-shirt into something that looked great. It was her New York style or something. "But you didn't answer my question," Dahlia added.

"About French or Spanish?"

Dahlia rolled her eyes. "Julie, Spanish meets at eight o'clock in the morning. I'm still in dreamland then. No, I meant the question about the cutest guy."

Julie went through the motions of glancing around the crowded room, but she didn't bother to stop and take a real look at anyone. Against the snaking lines of students circling choices in their course catalogs, and milling around the drab room, what stood out in her mind's eye was the picture of her and Matt snuggled in the hammock in her backyard one Saturday afternoon, poring over the catalog that had just arrived from Madison in the mail. "Dahlia, I have a boyfriend already," she said.

"So?" Dahlia asked as they moved closer to the front of the line. "He's a million miles away."

"A few hundred," Julie said with a touch of annoyance.

"Julie, I thought they gave me the smartest person in the freshman class for a roommate," Dahlia said. She tapped her head. "You think Matt expects you to purposely try and be miserable at college? Looking for the cutest boy is just a game. Come on, I'll start." Dahlia made a slow circle in place. She stopped abruptly as her gaze reached the door. "Him—just coming in. Mr. Rock Star with the incredible hair."

Julie looked at the guy with the long, flowing, curly mane of red-blond hair. "Yeah, he's pretty cute," she agreed. "But he secretly spends half the morning fussing over his hair. He'd absolutely die if his roommate found out."

Dahlia laughed. "Okay, so you pick someone better."

Julie looked around again, more carefully this time. Maybe if she picked someone out, Dahlia would quit prodding her and she could go back to her thoughts of Matt.

The guy up at the front of the line wasn't bad. But as she heard his voice come out in a thin whine, Julie changed her mind. Her eyes traveled down the line at the next table—the one for natural-science courses. She didn't even have to think about it—her eyes just seemed to stop on the guy with the light brown hair and the fine-featured face. In his jeans and polo shirt, sporting a pair of well-worn cowboy boots, she could see he was thin but nicely built. Julie felt herself blushing.

"Who?" Dahlia asked.

"Oh, all right," Julie whispered, "him." She

nodded in the guy's direction. "Reading that letter, or whatever it is. Okay?"

"More than okay," Dahlia said. "Second part of the game: Why don't you see if you can find out what he's taking, and sign up for one of his classes?"

Julie let out a sigh. "No way, Dahlia. I know what I'm signing up for, and I didn't come to college to meet guys." As if he felt their eyes on him, the boy in the cowboy boots looked up from his reading. As his gaze moved in their direction, Julie quickly turned away.

Dahlia shrugged. "To each her own," she said. "I hope your friend Matt knows what he's got."

"I think he does," Julie said. "I hope."

Julie sat at her desk, eyeing the phone on the wall of her little room. *No, Jules,* she told herself. She'd probably already spent her first week's paycheck on calls to Philly, and she hadn't even started her job in the dining hall yet.

She opened up one of the fresh notebooks she'd bought at Books and Things, carefully tore out a sheet of paper, and uncapped her favorite pen. *Dear Matt,* she wrote. *My first Friday night at college. Been here less than a week, and I miss you so much. Dahlia's out with her new boyfriend, Andy. The girl does move fast.* She put down her pen. Maybe that wasn't the right thing to say. She remembered how edgy Matt had gotten when she'd mentioned Dahlia and Andy and the whole subject of boys. But he'd said he wanted to hear about everything that was happening at school. Besides, *Julie* wasn't out with some guy she'd just met. She was sitting in her dorm room—alone. She continued writing.

Freshman orientation's almost over. The upperclassmen are starting to arrive. I was just starting to feel a little more comfortable here—getting to know everyone in the dorm and stuff. Now it feels like we're being invaded. There's one senior on my hall who's lived in Wilson every single year. She's all rah-rah about this dorm. If you saw the place, you wouldn't be able to believe it.

Julie leaned back in her chair for a moment and looked around. The room did look a little homier since she'd taped up some posters and put out her favorite photos. The snapshot of her and Matt at the Delaware River graced her desk —two happy, wet faces grinning at her from over her notebook. At the foot of her bed, so it would be the first thing and the last thing she saw every day, she'd hung a poster of one of Monet's flower paintings. Julie felt an overwhelming sense of calm every time she looked at its deep, tranquil purples and greens. She'd read that the paintings had their own special room in a tiny jewel of a museum in a park in Paris.

Paris. The course catalog said that Madison had a junior year abroad program there. Maybe Julie would have a chance to see the water lilies for herself. But as she looked back over at the picture of her and Matt, her heart fell. Paris? As if Madison, Ohio, weren't far enough away.

She glanced at the telephone again, then back down at her letter. *Classes start at the beginning of next week,* she wrote. *I'm taking journalism (yay, they let me into an upper-level course), Intro to Women's Lit, French, and Human Biology. Bio is five days a week! Maybe Marion from next door can help me with it. She's a total science whiz.*

Julie put her pen aside and reread the letter. Dahlia, boys, upperclassmen. A list of classes. Marion. She blew out a noisy breath of frustration and balled up the piece of paper.

She was excited about school, but why should Matt care about people he'd never met and a bunch of classes he was never going to take? Julie pushed her chair away from her desk and stood up. She walked over to the open window and leaned out. The night sky was huge over the cornfields and full of brilliant stars. The air had the pungent, sharp-sweet smell of summer as it turned into fall. Julie could hear a light breeze as it rustled the leaves of the trees. It was a perfect night, but all Julie felt was an ache in her chest.

If Matt were there, it would be different. She tried to imagine it. Matt at college? If Matt were there, well, for starters he'd probably be signed up for advanced rock climbing—not that Julie had seen any rocks around campus to climb—off-trail cycling, Campus Parties 101. He'd probably work on the social board, bringing bands out to Madison the way he did at the Fast Lane. Maybe he and Julie would be double-dating with Dahlia and Andy at that Barn and Grill place. Afterward, they'd go out into the middle of one of those fields Julie was looking at and gaze at the stars.

She felt a tingle go up and down her arms as she remembered picking out the constellations on one of their first real dates. They'd been in front of the triplex after seeing a movie. The Big Dipper and the Little Dipper had been shining brightly above them. "And see that cluster of six stars there?" Matt had asked. "That's the Seven Sisters. Don't ask," he'd added before she could say a thing. "I guess the seventh one took a wrong turn in the Milky Way."

Julie had given a bittersweet laugh. "Even stars have sisters who aren't there anymore," she'd said.

Matt had instantly folded her into a tight hug.

"Hey, I didn't mean to make you feel bad." He'd stroked her head softly with his palm.

"It's okay," Julie had answered. "The pain is something I'm going to have to live with."

She and Matt had stood in a silent embrace for a long time. "Listen, why don't we skip the ice cream and go for a ride?" Matt had finally suggested softly. "We could head out to the Poconos. The sky's so much clearer without any city lights nearby."

Julie remembered clutching on to him, her arms wrapped around his leather jacket as they rode into the crisp night. The bike's vibrations filled her body. The chill air rushed to meet her. Matt had taken her to the summit of a high, heavily forested mountain, the lights of the closest towns only little glittery specks way down in the distance. That was the night Julie had seen her first shooting star.

A rap on the dorm room door brought Julie back down to earth. "Who is it?" she asked, crossing through her side of the room to Dahlia's.

"Paul," said a muffled voice.

Julie opened the door. "Hi, Paul," she said. "Dahlia's not around."

"Oh." Paul frowned, peering in beyond her. "Well, do you have any idea where she is?"

Julie hesitated. "Uh—I'm not really sure," she said, crossing her fingers behind her back. She felt bad about lying to him, but it wasn't her job to tell him that Dahlia had already hooked up with somebody. Paul's long, thin face looked even longer. The guy had it big-time for Dahlia. But then again, who didn't? In less than a week, Julie was already getting used to having people say, "You mean the really incredible one with the long blond hair?" Or, "Oh, you're Dahlia's roommate?"

"Well, sorry to bother you," Paul said, shifting around on his lanky legs.

"It's okay. I wasn't really doing much," Julie said. "Just writing a letter to my boyfriend. The girls in the triple at the end of the hall are having a party—I was thinking of going down there in a little while. You can come if you want." She realized that it was nice to be talking to someone instead of sitting alone on her first Friday of college.

Paul bobbed his head. "Cool," he said.

"Come on in," Julie said, moving aside to let him through. "Have a soda or something first. Dahlia rented us one of these mini fridges." She nodded at the little boxlike refrigerator on the floor near Dahlia's bed. "We stocked up on drinks and munchies."

"Excellent. I'll have whatever you've got." Paul

61

came in and sat down cross-legged on the floor. Julie fished for a couple of Cokes, handing him one and cracking the tab on the other.

"So, what classes did you end up signing up for? Did you get that English course you wanted?" She pulled Dahlia's desk chair toward Paul and sat down.

"Yeah." Paul took a sip of Coke. "Kerouac, Ginsberg, Burroughs—cool dudes," he said.

"Good writers, too." Julie laughed. Sure, she'd rather be stargazing with Matt. But that wasn't why she'd left Philadelphia.

Six

❧

Dahlia threw on Andy's denim shirt, rolled up the sleeves, and buttoned it up. In the first weak, pink-gray strains of light coming in through Andy's window, she took a quick glance in the mirror and smoothed her hair. She could feel Andy watching her as she picked up the silver dress draped over his chair and her sling-back shoes.

He propped himself up in bed on one elbow. "Hey, beautiful, where are you going?"

Dahlia felt a thrill of warmth. She liked hearing Andy call her beautiful. "To my room to get some sleep," she whispered. She leaned down and gave him a moist kiss on the mouth. "I had a really fun time," she added. "Thanks."

"Me too," Andy said. His wavy blond hair was

rumpled and all he wore was a sleepy smile. Pretty cute.

"Room 103," Dahlia said. "Come visit, if you want," she said lightly.

"Definitely," Andy said. He yawned and lay back. "See you later."

"See you." Dahlia put her fingertips to her lips and blew him another kiss. Then she tiptoed through the outer room, where Andy's roommate was snoring away, the covers pulled up over his head.

She walked through the deserted halls of the dorm, sleepily dazed but happy. College was going to be a blast. No more watching TV alone up in the luxurious glass cage of her parents' penthouse. No more eating by herself in the Chinese restaurant down the block: *How is miss tonight? Does miss want something else?*

Yes, miss wanted something else, and now she had it. This year was going to be filled, every minute of it, with fun, friends, and lots of boys—a real big happy family of cool kids. As she made her way down the stairs Dahlia could still feel the warmth of Andy's body like a blanket of love around her. She came out of the stairwell and nearly bumped smack into Marion—that Kansas girl who was really from Ohio.

"Hi, Dahlia!" Marion chirped brightly. She was

clear-eyed, rested, and full of early-morning energy. It was like coming out of a dark, warm cave and being hit by a flood of sharp white light. Dahlia took a step backward.

"Oh, hi, Marion," she said, her voice thick and soft.

"So, you're an early riser, too!" Marion said. "You know, after getting up to do farm chores every day, I just can't get used to all this sleeping in. I wish classes started at six."

Six? Was the girl serious? Dahlia stared at her. She had on a pink, fluffy bathrobe and furry cow slippers.

"I was just about to wash up and get ready for breakfast," Marion went on. "Do you want to come?" Her eyes fell on the dress draped over Dahlia's arm and the shoes she carried. "Gee, what's the fancy outfit for?"

Dahlia ignored the question about the clothes. "Actually, Marion, I was just on my way to bed," she said. Marion's face went blank, then broke into a startled expression.

"Oh. Well, um . . . another time."

"Yeah, another time," Dahlia echoed. "Later." She gave Marion a little pat on her fluffy shoulder and beat it down the hall. "Time to milk the cows," she mumbled under her breath. Now she'd seen everything.

On the noteboard on the door to her room, she found a message scribbled. *I stopped by— Paul.* Without bothering to erase it, Dahlia let herself into the room, threw her dress and shoes on her chair, and fell right into bed.

Julie and Dahlia made it to the dining hall just as it was starting to empty out at the end of lunch. A few small groups of students lingered over cigarettes in the smoking section at the far end of the cavernous room. In the main section, only a couple of dozen people remained at the large, circular tables.

Outside, through a wall of plate-glass windows, Julie could see people ambling across Central Bowl—heading back to their dorms or over to Walker Main, the imposing ivy-covered stone building at the far end of the lawn that housed the mail room, the campus snack bar, and the Rathskeller—Madison's very own pub. Lots of kids sat out on the grass in groups, talking, reading, enjoying the sun. *It looks like a day at the beach but without the water,* Julie thought. Presiding over the whole scene, at the head of Central Bowl, was the library. A modern structure, it was an odd study in cement and glass and curved lines that looked as if it might take off any minute. The library wasn't seeing much action yet;

the entrance ramp was quiet. But come Monday, when classes started, Julie knew that would change fast.

She put her tray down near the window, sat down, and looked distastefully at what was on her plate: two pork chops that had been sitting in their own grease for most of lunch and a pile of lukewarm string beans. She'd helped herself to a dish of soft ice cream just as someone from the cleanup staff was about to remove the handles from the soft-serve machine.

"In case someone with a dire case of the munchies tries to break in for an afternoon snack," she had observed wryly to Dahlia. Now the ice cream was melting, making a puddle of chocolate running into vanilla in the bottom of her bowl.

Dahlia, still puffy-eyed from having just woken up, had a cup of black coffee and two slices of toast on her tray. "You should have seen her face when she realized I was just coming home for the night," she said, sitting down and taking a sip of her coffee. "I thought she might faint away in that fluffy bathrobe. Dead cows in the middle of the hall."

Julie couldn't help laughing, but she felt as if she ought to come to Marion's defense. "Dahlia, I know she's sort of, well—"

67

"A hayseed," Dahlia supplied.

Julie bit back her smile and shrugged. "Maybe. But she's really sweet. All excited about being here and stuff—and she's funny, too. I mean, I don't know if she means to be, but take last night, down in the triple. She was telling us all about her pet pigs—how she took care of them and named them, and how they had different personalities. Then she tells us the only problem is that at the end of the year they have to eat them." Suddenly, Julie looked down at her pork chops. She pushed them away and started on the soupy ice cream.

Dahlia was making a disgusted face. "Gross, Julie. You want to make me lose my appetite for this fabulous burnt toast?"

"Mine's not exactly a culinary wonder, either," Julie said. Good thing she and Dahlia had stuffed the refrigerator with goodies from Gibson's Bakery.

"Anyway, sweet or not, I didn't tell Marion where I'd been," Dahlia said, continuing with her story. "In a boy's room? In a boy's bed? Sleeping with him? I might have given the poor thing a heart attack."

Julie said nothing, stirring her spoon around in her ice cream. She thought about the package of condoms Dahlia had left lying on her desk.

What would Dahlia think if she knew that her own roommate had never spent the night with a boy? Well, not exactly. Julie and Matt had gone away overnight a few times, but no matter how hot and heavy it got, Julie had always found herself holding back at the last minute.

She thought about the camping trip they'd taken—it had been only the weekend before she left for school, but it seemed so far in the past, as if the miles between her and Matt had been converted into time. She remembered how they'd snuggled down inside the sleeping bags they'd zipped together, the wind howling through the trees outside the tent, the night air brisk with the close of summer. She remembered the feel of their arms around each other in the soft, quilted cocoon they'd shared, their light, gentle kisses giving way to deep, hungry ones.

Their bodies had melted closer and closer as she traced the ripple of his muscles under her fingertips, shivering at the soft touch of his hands over her body, their legs entwined, inhaling the scent of his moist skin, their breaths short and fast. With her lips and her hands she had explored his face, his body.

Slowly, tenderly, they had undressed each other until they were almost naked. Matt's chest had been warm against her; his hand had brushed her bare breast, skin against skin. He'd kissed the hollows of her neck, and then their mouths found each other again, their bodies pressing together as if they could make themselves one—falling, falling into a place where time didn't exist, where nothing existed but their lips, their tongues, their hands, their bodies . . .

"Julie," Matt had whispered, pushing at the elastic of her panties.

Julie had wanted him to keep going. But as Matt started to remove the little remaining clothing they had on, she'd felt herself drawing back, away from him.

"Why, Julie?" Matt had whispered. "It feels right, us together." Julie had taken several deep breaths, her pulse beating through her body. "Don't be afraid," he'd said.

Was she? Was she afraid? She knew she loved Matt, wanted to share everything with him. But something had held her back. This feeling in her body, in her heart—it was so out of control. Out of control, like Mary Beth used to be. "We're going to be apart for so long," she'd said to Matt. "But if we're meant to be, there'll be plenty of time."

Matt had let go of her, his fast, heated breathing slowly returning to normal. "Jules," he'd said after a few minutes. "I'm not going to pretend I don't want you."

Julie had taken his hand and brought it to her lips. She'd hated to push him away like that. She loved him so much. . . .

"Knock, knock," Dahlia was saying. "Anyone in there? Where are you, Julie?"

Julie felt herself turning about a dozen shades of red.

"Thinking about Matt for the millionth time today," Dahlia said, answering her own question. "Julie, you really want to spend all your time day-dreaming about someone who's not around?"

Julie gazed out the dining hall window with unfocused eyes. "I just want to be with him," she said, her mind still half with Matt.

"Well, you picked a hell of a way to do it," Dahlia commented.

Julie came back to reality with a crash. She sighed loudly, spooning up a big bite of liquid ice cream.

Dahlia reached across the table and jostled Julie's arm affectionately. "I don't mean to bum you out. I just think it's time we got you out a little more. You know, the old college try and all that. Look at all those people out there." She nodded at the kids hanging out on Central Bowl. "They're here for the college experience—the best four years of their lives. You don't want to miss out, do you?"

Julie shrugged. "Hey, I went to the party at the triple last night. Your friend Paul came around looking for you—I took him with me."

"You did? That was nice of you. Thanks, Julie."

"Sure. He really seemed to hit it off with Bob and Scott."

"Who?" Dahlia asked.

"You know—those guys across the hall who are always blasting the Grateful Dead? Anyway, it was a pretty good party. You should have been there."

Dahlia grinned. "I was having my own kind of party," she said.

"I bet," Julie answered. At least Dahlia wasn't going to miss out on the college experience.

Seven

❦

Julie had a major case of the jitters. She was walking quickly across Central Bowl toward the low, modern building called Fischer, where her first class was about to meet. In her gray canvas shoulder bag with all the pockets was a brand-new notebook labeled *Journalism* and several new pens and freshly sharpened pencils. In some ways it was like any other first day of school. She had on a new tartan skirt, she'd shined her loafers, and she'd put on some makeup, which she usually did only on special occasions. She'd woken up early, way before her alarm went off, her stomach fluttery with anticipation.

But that day there had been no breakfast with her family, no one to send her off to school and tell her to have a nice day. That day she'd showered in the bathroom down the hall while Gwen from the triple sang in the stall next to hers. Then she'd sneaked back into her room to get dressed as Dahlia dove under the covers—she didn't have any classes until eleven. She'd bumped into Marion and Susan leaving the dorm and they'd all gone to breakfast together—they were even more nervous than she was.

Now Julie was entering the stark, white halls of Fischer with a swarm of other students. College was really about to begin. Orientation was officially over. Finally.

Julie had thought about Dahlia's little lecture on missing out on all the college fun, and she'd let her roommate coax her into two parties over the weekend. Saturday night they'd gone to Zeke —"You know, that jock dorm," Dahlia had said— and Sunday night there had been a smaller party in someone's dorm room over on South Campus. It wasn't that Julie hadn't had fun. She'd danced until late enough at the Zeke party, first with Andy's roommate, Gregg, and then with a few of the other guys from her dorm. She'd talked to almost everybody at the South party. But she couldn't help feeling that the parties weren't so different from the ones she'd gone to back home, except that no one had to be home at a certain time—and except that Matt wasn't with her.

Julie felt a sizzle of nerves as she walked into

Fischer 209. Most of the kids there were upper-classmen. She felt their eyes on her as she chose a seat—not too far back, but not right in the front row, either. She took out her notebook and a pen and put them on the desk—a shelflike extension of the chair that curved around in front of her. She wished she'd called Matt before class, just to hear his voice and have him send her good luck, but he was probably still asleep. Besides, it would have made six phone calls since she arrived. They hadn't even tried to stick to the once-a-week rule.

Inside the front cover of her journalism note-book she'd tucked an issue of *The Flyer,* her high school paper. She'd written the lead story in it, a carefully researched article about the successes and failures of neighborhood recycling programs. She'd worked hard on it and hoped that Professor Copeland—whoever he was—would want to know what kind of writing his students had done in the past.

Julie glanced around the room. Two seats away, with an empty seat between them, was the boy with the long red-blond hair whom Dahlia had pointed out at registration—the one Julie imagined secretly tending to his hair.

The boy looked over at her, and she realized

she'd been staring. "Hi," she said, a little embarrassed. She toyed with her pen.

"Hey," the boy said. "Ready for Killer Copeland?" He ran a hand through his hair.

"Killer?" Julie raised her eyebrows.

The boy gave her a long look. "Freshman, huh?"

Julie nodded, feeling even more nervous than she had when she'd walked in.

"Copeland's got kind of a rep on campus," the boy explained. "Brilliant, but—" His eyes swiveled to the door.

In strode speak-of-the-devil himself, a wiry little man half hidden under a bushy dark beard. He didn't look terribly imposing. But everyone seemed to sit up, straighten the books on their desks, or brush away some nonexistent speck of dust on their clothing. The kids who came in after he did scrambled to sit down as he paced in front of the class. The tension in the room increased more and more with his back-and-forth motion. Julie waited for something to happen.

The bell echoed through the building, and Professor Copeland sprang. "Journalism," he said, hurling the word out at his students. "News. What are they?"

Julie recoiled under Professor Copeland's surprise attack. Silence swelled in the room.

76

Professor Copeland stopped his pacing abruptly and whirled toward the class. "Yes?" he said, his eyes scanning each row of new faces. "You, there." He pointed at a guy in the front row.

The teacher gave him almost no time to collect his thoughts before his eyes were moving toward his next target. Julie watched his gaze cutting across the row in front of her, then her row. Closer. "All right, then, you."

Oh, my God, Julie thought. *He's looking right at me.* She made herself meet his dark, unreadable eyes, but her mind was a white screen of panic.

"Yes, you, Miss—"

"Miller," Julie managed to get out. She swallowed hard and made herself breathe normally. She wasn't going to let anyone spoil her first few minutes of college. Even a professor. "Ms. Miller," she amended, emphasizing the *Ms.*

Professor Copeland's face lit up and Julie started to relax. "Ms.," he said, managing to inflate the word with his delight. "Ah, yes, Ms. Miller. Very well, Ms. Miller. Tell me, then, why is it Ms.? Is it because it's fashionable, or does it go deeper than that? Do you know the history of the word you've chosen as part of your own name?"

Julie felt her heart sink. That was why he was smiling. Because she'd played right into his

77

hands. She'd tried to stand up for herself and Professor Copeland had shot her right down.

"Well, Ms. Miller?" he said. "We're waiting. You are in a class that's all about questions—and answers. What's your view about the relationship between language and women's rights? Do you know the current facts and cases pertaining to the issue?"

Julie couldn't think straight. He kept firing questions at her. Before she'd had a chance to formulate the answer to one, he'd shot off another. Besides, her anger was jumbling all the words that came into her head.

"Or are you simply Ms. Miller?" Professor Copeland asked. "These are the types of things a real journalist needs to have a handle on. We must know all the angles. Are you still interested in becoming a journalist, Ms. Miller? Can you manage it? Can any of you?"

Julie let out a silent breath as Professor Copeland opened his personal attack out onto the class in general. She felt like a balloon deflating.

"So for those of you who think that a journalist need ask only who, what, when, where, and why, there's the door," Professor Copeland said dramatically.

Julie didn't even dare look up at him. If no one was moving toward the door, it was probably because they were all frozen to their seats in fear. Was this what college was all about? Total humiliation on the first day of class?

Julie could only half listen as Professor Copeland went on. She thought about her copy of *The Flyer,* tucked neatly into her notebook, and about all the praise and encouragement she'd gotten from Mr. Ben-Ari, the staff adviser to the paper. She thought about her straight-A average in high school. And how she'd just assumed that she'd continue to do well in college. Sure, she had doubts and worries about coming to Madison, but whether she'd be a top student was not among them. Until now.

Now Professor Copeland's string of questions spawned only more questions in Julie's mind. Why hadn't she tossed the right answers back into her professor's face? Why hadn't she shown him that she was good enough for his class? Why had she let him make her feel so small?

Back home, everyone knew that Julie was one of the best students at school, and it had always been important to her. She knew it had something to do with Mary Beth, something to do with the fact that her sister was the one everyone noticed, the one who spoke right up and said what was on her mind, the one her friends followed, the wild one, the one to try everything first. But

Julie was the one they stopped to listen to, the one who knew the right answers, the model student and daughter who made her parents proud.

In a few brief moments, Professor Copeland had destroyed that strength and confidence. Stinging tears rose to Julie's eyes. She felt as if everyone else in the class must be stealing glances at her, feeling sorry for her but relieved that they hadn't been the professor's first victim. Mary Beth might not have been the world's best student, but there was no way she would have put up with the treatment Julie had just received. When Professor Copeland had pointed out the door, Mary Beth would have marched right out. But not before telling him exactly what she thought of him.

Julie wished she'd done the same. Instead, she sat in her seat until class was over, struggling to keep her tears in check. When the bell rang, she was the first one out into the hall. The faces around her blurred as she let go and cried. She ran through the hall and down the crowded stairwell, just trying to put as much distance as possible between her and Fischer 209. She didn't stop running until she was out the door of the building, all the way across Central Bowl, and standing in front of the telephone bank in Walker Main.

* * *

"Jules? Hey, wow!" said Matt's sleepy, throaty morning voice. "I was just dreaming about you. Hey, Jules? Julie, what's the matter?"

Julie was sobbing into the phone as soon as she heard his warm, dream-smudged words. "Oh, Matt. I'm sorry to wake you up, but the worst thing just happened . . ." She wiped at her eyes and nose with the back of her hand.

Matt's voice was suddenly wide awake. "Julie, are you all right?" Fear pulsed through the telephone line.

"I'm fine," she said quickly, realizing that she'd made it sound as if she'd been run over by a train. A train named Professor Copeland. "It's just that I had my first class and it was so awful." The story came pouring out in a flood of tears and relief. "He made me feel like such a jerk," she finally concluded.

"Come on, Julie, come on," Matt crooned as if he were there with her, holding her and stroking her hair. "You know the jerk was this Copeland guy, not you," he said reasonably.

Julie sniffled into the telephone. "Yeah, I know it, but he embarrassed me in front of the whole class. And it was, like, my first two seconds of school."

Matt laughed softly. "I think you ought to write your first article for the Madison paper,

Jules. 'Exalted Professor Bullies Prize Student for No Good Reason.'"

"You mean Ms. Prize Student," Julie said, her sniffles giving way to a little giggle. "Right. I'm sure that would stand me in even better stead with the guy."

"Well, then, maybe you should duke it out with him," Matt said. "It sounds like that's what he needs."

"Yeah, I could probably whup him, too," Julie said. "The guy's totally scrawny and about four feet tall."

"Which may say something about why he needs to pick on people," Matt commented.

"Not people, Matt. Me," Julie said. She felt better just getting it off her chest and poking fun at it. "So, how about you, sleepyhead? What were you dreaming, anyway?"

"I don't know exactly. Something about you coming into the club and sneaking up on me, and I was so happy because I'd thought you were gone. . . ."

Julie sighed. "I wish it were true. I wish I could just pop in on you whenever I wanted. I don't know. With teachers like Professor Copeland, it hardly seems worth it."

"Jules, it's one class," Matt said. "The rest of them will go better."

"They'd have to." Julie laughed. "Speaking of which, I should get going. My French class starts in—" She glanced at the clock on the wall behind her. "Now! Look, I'll call you later, okay?"

"I'll be waiting," Matt said. "Don't forget. I love you, Julie."

"Me, too," Julie said. She made a kissing sound into the phone. "Thanks for listening to me."

"Anytime," Matt said.

They exchanged good-byes and Julie hung up. As she turned to go she spotted the cute guy with the cowboy boots, the guy she'd picked out at registration, at the phone next to her. Her face got instantly warm.

"Hi, Allison?" she couldn't help overhearing him say. "Hey, finally! I've been trying to call for the past four days! Where've you been? It's great to hear your voice. . . ."

So her mystery man was a casualty of home-town heartbreak, too! Julie walked away to give him some privacy. She wondered if he'd heard her talking to Matt and knew he wasn't the only one missing someone back home. With everyone she'd met so far either pairing off or looking to pair off, it was nice to find out she had some company.

* * *

"At least things improved after journalism," Julie said to Dahlia as she dug into a bag of cheese popcorn. They were sitting on the floor of Julie's side of the room, a late-night picnic of sodas and junk food spread out between them. "Madame DuPrès spent practically the whole class explaining how to make the perfect omelette. At first I thought that she's, like, this crackpot, but then I realized I'd learned all this really basic household vocabulary. After that, biology was kind of, well, impersonal—it's in this huge lecture hall and the teacher has to use a mike, but I think it's going to be pretty interesting."

Dahlia slurped her diet Coke. "So that just leaves that girls' class tomorrow?"

Julie rolled her eyes. "Dahlia, it's Women's Lit. It's not some girls' class. You know, there might even be some guys who are in it."

"Yeah? How many? One? Two?"

Julie laughed. "Is that how you're judging your classes? What percent is guys?"

"Only if they're cute," Dahlia said, smiling. "English 101? Ooh, baby. And the teacher? Professor Yorowitz? He's pretty good-looking, too, in that shabby corduroy intellectual kind of way."

Julie laughed. "Not to go putting labels on people, right? Oh, hey, speaking of cute, remember that guy from registration?"

"The rock star with the hair?"

Julie shook her head. "No, but as a matter of fact, that guy's in journalism with me."

"He is?" Dahlia scarfed down a handful of popcorn.

"Yeah. I sat next to him. He's nice. I feel kind of bad about saying that he must spend all that time fussing over his hair—even though it's true." Julie giggled. "But actually, I was talking about the other guy. The one in the cowboy boots."

"Oh. Your guy."

Julie felt herself blushing. "He's not my guy. No way. What I wanted to tell you was that I heard him on the phone when I was calling Matt, and he has a hometown sweetheart, too."

Dahlia shrugged. "Too bad."

"Too bad? Why? I thought you really liked Andy."

"Dah-ling," Dahlia intoned theatrically. "One is never enough. But I didn't mean *me* and Mr. Cowboy Boots. I meant *you*."

Julie felt a touch of irritation. "Dahlia . . ."

"I know," she replied. "Matt."

"Well, yes," Julie said, feeling a little defensive. "Is there something wrong with really being in love with someone?"

Dahlia stretched her legs out. "No," she said

with a sigh. "I mean, of course I'm totally envious."

"You are?" Julie felt a tickle of surprise. "You could have most of the guys on campus falling all over you."

Dahlia grinned. "That sounds like fun. But it couldn't compare to, well . . . to true love."

Julie heard the hint of longing in Dahlia's voice. "Then how come you think I should forget about Matt?" she asked. "I don't get it."

Dahlia frowned. "You're right. You don't get it. No way I'm saying you should give the guy up. I just think you need to let yourself have some fun here. I mean, it's gonna be four long and lonely years otherwise."

"You mean, like, two-time him?" Julie asked, her words coming out as if they tasted sour.

Dahlia gave a wry laugh. "You think I'm an evil woman."

Julie laughed, too. "No. I just—I don't know. I guess I don't understand. I mean, it's not only a matter of principle. I don't want anyone besides Matt." She took a deep breath. "Even though it would be easier if I did."

"You mean because he's not here," Dahlia supplied.

"Well, that. Definitely that," Julie said. "But

also because of my folks. They're so against us being together."

"Because of what happened to your sister?" Dahlia asked. Julie had started to tell her the story a few nights earlier.

"Yeah." Julie nodded. "At least, that was why at first. Now it's as if they're just so used to disapproving that it's automatic, you know? They won't even get to know what Matt's really like. Fortunately, my brother thinks he's the greatest thing since two wheels. And Mary Beth—she liked him, too." Julie felt a tug of sadness. "She used to go out with his friend Mark. He was in the car, too. . . ." Tears welled up.

Dahlia reached over and touched her arm. "Hey," she said softly. "It stinks. I know. I mean, I don't know, really, but I can imagine. I used to wish I had a sister—or a brother. I still do sometimes."

Julie suddenly felt selfish. Dahlia was lonely. Popular, beautiful Dahlia, who seemed to have everything, had grown up feeling all alone. Julie suddenly understood why it was so important for her to be surrounded by admirers. "Well, a roommate's sort of like a sister," she volunteered.

Dahlia smiled broadly. "Yeah," she said. "I guess that's true."

Eight

❧

First class, first worm, first love! Marion thought, trying to steady her scalpel enough to slice open the earthworm on her lab table.

"Here, you want me to do it?" asked Fred Fryer, brushing her hand with his as he reached for the scalpel.

Marion felt an electric zing go through her as she let him take it. "I'm sorry," she said. "It's just that—" What? That she couldn't concentrate on Squiggly when Fred was standing so close to her? That she could smell his soap and his aftershave mixing in with the formaldehyde? That she'd noticed the gold flecks in his brown eyes?

"Yeah, they're kind of slimy," Fred said, expertly splitting open the worm's segmented skin.

"Oh, it's not that," Marion said quickly. "I mean, yeah, they are slimy, but the worms in my barn at home are way bigger and slimier than this one."

"*Wormus longius slimius,* huh?" Fred said.

"Extra *longius.*" Marion giggled. "This one's just a little guy. But I guess I'm nervous. First day of class and everything." "Everything" being Fred, of course.

Fred carefully pinned the split skin flat to the dissection board. The worm's organs rested in a long cylinder on top of it, like a roll of tobacco laid out on a piece of cigarette paper. "Well, I've dissected my share of earthworms before," he said. "But I'm more used to them dead than alive —being from the middle of Cincinnati and all. I mean, you can't go digging 'em up under the sidewalk. Here, you want to find the hearts? There are five of them, according to the manual."

Marion had to force herself to concentrate. And not on Fred. *Hearts,* she told herself, studying the worm. Her own heart was beating extra hard. "Oh, yeah, these five tubelike things here," she said, indicating them with a slender metal pointer.

"Pretty convenient, huh?" Fred commented. "If these guys get a terminal case of heartbreak, they still have four hearts left."

Marion felt herself blushing, as if Fred were talking about her. They flagged the hearts with blue-headed dissection pins. "So, what was it like growing up on a farm?" Fred asked, putting in the final pin.

"Well, it's a great way to really learn about animals and plants and stuff," she said. *Great. I sound like I'm having my interview for college. Why growing up on a farm makes me ready for your school.*

But Fred sounded interested. "I'll bet," he said enthusiastically. "I had to get all my information secondhand, from my father," he said. "He's a geneticist."

"Really?" Marion was impressed. "He invents new species and stuff? Invasion of the superhumans?"

"Well, not quite," Fred confessed. "More like he tries to grow strawberries that don't bruise when they're shipped or oranges with fewer seeds. Things like that. But he does it all in the lab."

Fred turned to consult the dissection manual and Marion snuck another look at him. He had an interesting face, with a smattering of freckles across his nose and thick red-brown hair. He was only a little taller than she was. Some girls might think that was too short, but if he and Marion were standing face-to-face, he'd be the perfect height for a good-night kiss.

90

"Next we have to find the crop," Fred said. "It's this bulge below the heart where food is stored."

"Oh, yeah. Like the worm's personal pantry," Marion joked. "What do you think's in there? Dirt à la mode?"

"Or mud with house special sauce?" Fred said.

Marion couldn't believe she was talking and laughing with a boy so easily. And it was only the first day of class. She smiled to herself as she found the crop and flagged it with an orange pin. Would she one day be telling her children, "Daddy and I fell in love over the guts of an earthworm"?

Julie stood behind the dining hall counter in her white apron, her hair pulled back in a ponytail, rereading Matt's letter. *Took advantage of the incredible weather and rode down to the Jersey shore to do some body surfing,* he'd written. *Stopped for clams and corn at our place. Where were you?*

Every few minutes, Julie stopped to check the steel-and-glass shelves in front of her and make sure they were stocked with a choice of french fries, peas, beets, and succotash, each in a small, shallow white bowl. A continuous stream of kids pushed trays along the service line, grabbing plates of food from the shelves and counters. One huge guy—he had to be a football player—had managed to heap just about everything they served onto his tray. Julie wondered if he ate like that at every meal. A tall, gangly girl had selected only white foods, Julie noticed: yogurt, cottage cheese, rice, and vanilla cake. Weird.

"Don't you have any mashed potatoes today?" the girl asked Julie.

Julie tried not to look at her too strangely. "Just what's there," she said, going back to her letter. She was accompanied by the sound of clanging utensils and dishes and a steady roar of voices. The smell was not exactly appetizing, but she was getting used to it.

Sorry to hear about your tough time in journalism, Matt had written. *I'm sure you're acing everything else.* He'd drawn a little picture in the margin of a poker hand with four aces and one joker. Julie ran her fingers over it and giggled.

"Hey, girl, I said beets, not fries," said a familiar voice in line.

"Dahlia!" Her roommate had stuck her whole head on the top shelf, resting her chin in between the dishes of vegetables. Her painted red lips were stretched back in a crazy grin. "You look like a demented cabbage," Julie said.

"Well, I had to do something to get your attention. Caught you pining away again, huh?"

"Not pining," Julie protested. "Just reading a letter."

"From Matty-boy," Dahlia said with certainty. "How many times have you read it?"

Julie laughed. "A dozen? Two dozen? Look, he drew me pictures." She passed the letter over to Dahlia.

Dahlia took a quick look. "Cute, Julie. Very cute. You two win the long-distance-couple-of-the-week award." She passed the letter back.

"Just the week?" Julie said. "I was hoping we could do better than that." She put the letter up next to her face and affected her best beauty-pageant smile. "And in the four-hundred-miles-apart category, over one week and still madly in love: Julie and Matt. Let's give them a round of applause for making it this far, ladies and gentlemen."

"You're hopeless." Dahlia laughed. "Hey, did you notice the megabargain I picked up at Secondhand Rose?" She stretched her arms out and turned slowly, showing off her dark green flower-print dress with a tight bodice and full skirt. As she came back around she nearly socked the guy in back of her in the stomach. He gave her a dirty look and carried his tray around her. "And check it out. Real faux pearls." She fingered the choker around her neck.

"Speaking of hopeless," Julie said.

"Ah, excuse me, Julie. Sorry to interrupt the fashion show, but there's a whole line in back of your friend," said a deep, stern voice from the doorway of the kitchen.

Flustered, Julie looked over her shoulder at Mr. Raymond, her boss. "Oh, sorry, sir." She turned back to Dahlia. "Look, I'll see you later."

Dahlia raised an eyebrow conspiratorially. "Got to keep handing over those yummy little dishes," she said. "Give me some of those lovely overcooked peas, please."

"Dahlia, it's self-service," Julie whispered back.

"Ooh. Tough job, Julie. For this you need to be in college?"

Julie giggled. "Just get out of here, okay?"

Dahlia skipped the vegetables altogether and picked up her tray. "Okay. See you."

"See you," Julie said. She folded up Matt's letter and tucked it into the back pocket of her jeans. She didn't want to have to write back to him with the news that she'd gotten fired her first week on the job. Besides, she had the whole letter memorized already.

Nine

❧

The other side of college life. Dahlia was stretched out on her bed with her chemistry book. *What a drag.* Back to school—and in such a major way. She couldn't believe how much work they expected freshmen to do. It was less than a week into the semester, and she had already managed to fall behind in three of her four classes—the fourth being Theater Improv, in which they hadn't been assigned any homework yet.

The first shell of any atom can hold up to two electrons, Dahlia read lazily. *The second up to eight.* Who cared? She continued reading without trying to memorize any of the numbers. *If the outer shell of an atom is not complete, it will bond with another atom, sharing electrons to complete its outer shell and forming a molecule.*

Dahlia pushed the book aside and closed her

eyes. She wouldn't have minded a little bonding just then, but Andy was at swim practice. Julie had gone to the library with a humongous stack of books, and the rest of the hall was pretty quiet —except for the constant thump of Bob and Scott's Grateful Dead. Was there life after orientation? Not much, apparently.

Dahlia got up and opened her door. Bob and Scott's music spilled into the room. She wasn't all that excited about listening to the same album for the tenth time that day, but at least with the door open there was a chance that someone walking by the room might distract her from her work. Paul, Marion, anybody. She went back to her chemistry text, keeping one eye on the hall. Molecular structure. Maybe she should have taken Physics for Poets—or Rocks for Jocks, as they called Geology 101.

Finally there was some movement outside her doorway. Dahlia looked up to see a tall, muscle-bound, gorgeous guy with sandy-colored hair walking by. She almost fell off the bed. He couldn't have looked better in a dream. *Oh my God, who was that incredible creature?* As the view through the doorway went back to boring again, she stumbled to her feet and jogged over to see where he was going. His broad back was just disappearing into the triple at the end of the hall.

Did one of those girls go out with that Adonis? Which one? Amanda? She was okay, but she looked like a strawberry-coated elf. Gwendolyn? She'd met some guy in her black studies class whom she'd fallen head over heels for. Dahlia had just seen them together in the dining hall that morning. That left Sarah. But hadn't she and Marion the Milkmaid spent orientation week commiserating about finding Mr. Right at Madison?

Dahlia couldn't stand the suspense. She quickly put on a fresh coat of lipstick, ran a brush through her hair, and went down to the triple.

"Oh, hi, Dahlia," Sarah said, when she opened the door. Dahlia could see the guy hanging out on the couch. *Yes!* she thought. He was as cute as she'd thought from that first glimpse of him.

"Hey, Sarah. You up to anything?" she asked. "I sort of need a study break. Oops, sorry. I didn't know you had company."

"It's okay. Come on in," Sarah said. She stepped aside so Dahlia could get through. The triple was arranged like a suite, with one big bedroom for all three of the girls and an even bigger outer living room, which had quickly become the hangout for the entire hall. "There's some cake left over from Susan's birthday," Sarah offered.

Marion's roommate, Susan, had turned eighteen a couple of days earlier, and everyone on the hall had chipped in for a chocolate cake from Gibson's with a candy violin on top. It had been pretty good, but there was something more delicious in the room that Dahlia had her sights on. She flashed the guy on the couch her most dazzling smile. How had Sarah snagged this total babe?

"Husband?" she asked Sarah, her eyes fixed on the guy's perfect, even-featured face.

"Very funny, Dahlia." Both she and the guy started laughing. "Try brother. This is Tim," Sarah said.

Dahlia's smile got even bigger. "Hi," she said, not taking her eyes off him.

"Tim, Dahlia from down the hall," Sarah said.

He had an intriguing smile, with one corner of his mouth going up while the other went down. "Oh, yeah," he said. "With the little red car. I saw you driving around the other day."

"Tim's one of Madison's star football players," Sarah said proudly.

"Sarah, don't embarrass me." Tim was still looking at Dahlia. "We haven't won a game in two seasons."

"Well," Dahlia said saucily, "maybe your luck's about to change." She went over and sat down next to him on the couch. Up close, she could see that his deep-set eyes were blue-green and that he hadn't shaved that morning. "What position do you play?" She didn't know anything about football—except that Tim was built like a football player.

"Halfback," Tim said.

Dahlia made her eyes wide, as if she were impressed. Not that she had the slightest idea what a halfback did. "And you're a junior, right?"

Tim nodded. "Right. I see my sister's been talking about me," he said, but he didn't take his eyes off Dahlia.

"Um, about that chocolate cake," Sarah said loudly, as if announcing that she was still there.

"Oh, yeah, sure. I'll have a sliver," Dahlia said, looking straight back into Tim's eyes. "I have a huge sweet tooth."

Tim grinned. She grinned back at him. "I go for spicy myself," he said.

Oh, my God. The guy is too hot, Dahlia thought. "So, do you live in this dorm, too?" she asked, already planning a visit that didn't include his sister as a chaperone.

"Nah." Tim shook his head. "Living in a room that's like a shoebox gets to you after a while. I did my time in the dorms for two years."

Dahlia laughed. "Yeah, I know what you mean, and I've been here only two weeks. I don't even have a phone on my side of the room. So, what's your solution?"

"Oh, I live off campus," Tim said. "In a big old house on North Main Street I share with a bunch of friends."

All of a sudden, a paper plate with a slice of chocolate cake was being waved under Dahlia's nose. "A bunch of friends," Sarah echoed. "And his girlfriend," she added pointedly.

Dahlia took the chocolate cake. His girlfriend? Come on. There was no way she'd imagined the sparks that were flying between her and Tim. She looked up at Sarah's dark expression. Yeah, his sister had noticed the flirtation, too. Well, maybe it was okay. After all, Andy was sort of her boyfriend these days. So she and Tim were in the same situation.

She looked back up at him. He was still grinning at her with a glimmer in his blue-green eyes. It didn't seem as if having a girlfriend was worrying him, either.

Julie felt as though her dorm room had been transformed into a warehouse. She couldn't believe the number of boxes that had been crammed into their little divided double. Most of them were piled up on Dahlia's side, but some had overflowed into her half. Good thing the dorm director had been around to let the delivery people in, or she and Dahlia would have had to haul all the stuff over from the mail room. "What in the world is in all of them?" she asked in amazement. If she'd packed up every single thing she owned, she wouldn't have had a third as much.

Dahlia shrugged. "Clothes, mostly. You know —stuff I got from Daddy's store. There's some other things, too. Coffeepot, toaster oven—I know we're not supposed to have them, but they'll be great."

Julie squeezed by the towers of boxes and plunked down on Dahlia's unmade bed. "You know, we do have a kitchen down the hall, although I think the stove's got prehistoric crusty stuff on it," she said.

"That's why we need the toaster oven," Dahlia said. "Oh, and the most important thing. My CD player's in here somewhere." Dahlia tapped the boxes, as if that might offer a clue to their contents. "We can finally give Bob and Scott and the Grateful Dead some competition. Hmm. It's this box, maybe. No. No, this one's my down comforter. Good. I can give you your sleeping bag back."

Except there's not going to be anywhere to put it, Julie thought. Maybe she should go away for a few hours and let Dahlia figure out where to put everything while she was away. Or make that a few days.

Dahlia continued to walk around, opening the tops of some of the boxes and looking to see what was inside. "Posters, camera, video camera, TV," she announced.

"Oh, my God, Dahlia. A video camera?"

"Yeah, a video camera," Dahlia said, sounding defensive. "To memorialize our days of glory."

"To memorialize . . ." Julie echoed. Some people around the dorm said Dahlia was as spoiled as they came. For one guilty second, Julie found herself agreeing. Then she remembered the conversation they'd had at the beginning of the week—the one in which Dahlia had confided her loneliness. Dahlia had a lot of things. But not necessarily what counted, Julie thought. As she stared at the mountains of boxes there was a knock on their door.

"Who is it?" Dahlia called out.

"Delivery," came the muffled answer.

"I don't believe it!" Julie said as Dahlia went for the door. "The kitchen sink is the only thing you left home." All she could see from behind the boxes was Dahlia's long blond hair hanging down her back as she opened the door.

"Oh, wow!" she heard Dahlia exclaiming.

"That's so sweet of Daddy. Look what came with all the boxes!"

A man's low voice spoke. Julie couldn't quite make out what he was saying.

"Oh, not with the boxes?" Dahlia said. "They're not from Daddy. Figures. He's way too busy to go out of his way for me." There was a bitter note in her voice, but it didn't last long. "Well, who cares?" Dahlia said breezily. "I'd rather have them be from some mysterious secret admirer."

Julie got up from the bed and made her way around the boxes. She caught her breath when she saw what Dahlia was talking about. A short young man stood in the doorway with a magnificent bouquet of roses. They were round, huge flowers in full bloom—white, red, and every shade of pink in between. "Oh, Dahlia, they're beautiful," she exclaimed.

"Dahlia?" the delivery man said, his brow furrowed. "I'm looking for a Julie." He consulted a slip of paper. "Julie Miller."

Julie felt a surge of love and warmth for Matt. But it was tempered by Dahlia's flat, disappointed "oh."

"Hey, we'll share them," Julie said, taking the bouquet and breathing in its perfume. "I'm sure Matt wouldn't mind." She tipped the delivery man and then set the flowers on top of one of Dahlia's boxes. They were exquisite.

"I don't know why I figured they were for me," Dahlia said. "I thought maybe Andy—or Tim Pike . . ." She didn't finish her sentence.

Julie felt a funny pang of sympathy for Dahlia. She was surrounded by a truckload of possessions, and yet she was staring longingly at the bouquet of flowers. Julie gave her an impulsive little hug, not bothering to remind her that Tim Pike was taken, anyway.

"Well, they are beautiful," Dahlia said.

"Aren't they?" The flowers, arranged in a simple, wide-mouthed glass vase, were like the colors of a desert sunrise against the pale brown boxes. Julie noticed that nestled in the petals of the deepest crimson rose was a small white card. She inhaled deeply as she bent down to take it.

Not as beautiful as you, it read. *Love, Matt.*

The sweetness of Matt's roses—and his love— filled the room. He might be far away, but Julie suddenly felt that she was the luckiest person in the world. She wouldn't trade Matt's phone calls and flowers and notes of love for anything. Certainly not for a penthouse full of great clothes and a horde of admirers. Julie didn't want anyone but Matt—couldn't imagine anyone but Matt. And she had him. Even though they were four hundred miles apart.

There he was again. The cute guy with the long-distance girlfriend named Allison. Julie stole a look at him across the long, polished oak library table. His head was bowed over the notebook he was writing in, a lock of light brown hair falling over his forehead. Julie wondered what he was working on with such concentration.

She glanced down at her own nearly blank paper and let out a noisy sigh. *Obituary,* she'd written at the top of the page. She hadn't gotten any further. It figured that Professor Copeland would have them write an obituary for their first assignment. Julie guessed it was just to make sure no one started feeling too positive in his class. But she didn't need to write an obituary for that. He'd been making an example of Julie all week. And not a very good example.

She wished she could just forget about journalism and Professor Copeland. *Do some other assignment,* she told herself. Her bio homework was finished, though. And the language lab was closed for the night. And she was already all caught up in her reading for Women's Lit. That left the obituary.

"Freshman Dies of Humiliation," Julie thought,

imagining the headline of her own obituary as she leaned back in her chair with a sour chuckle. She saw Allison's boyfriend look over at her. She swallowed the chuckle and smiled at him. He smiled back—a nice, open smile. "Tough time in the library," Julie explained.

"I hear you," he said. "Happening spot to spend Friday night, huh?"

"Really. Be still, my beating heart," Julie cracked.

A girl at the end of the table shushed them from behind a pile of books. The guy looked at Julie, shrugged, and moved his things over so that he was directly across from her. "Big paper?" he asked.

"Not exactly," Julie said. "An obituary, actually."

"Oh, hey, being in the library on a Friday night's not that bad, is it?" he asked.

Julie rolled her eyes and laughed. "Not my obituary. But it feels that way." She told the boy about her shaky start in Professor Copeland's class. "I really want to ace the first assignment, but somehow that just makes it harder to get started. I mean, how much can I say about the guy, anyway? He died. And then what?"

"Sounds like your professor's not worth

making such an effort for," he commented. It was something Matt might say.

"He's not," Julie agreed. "But I guess I feel like I have to prove something to him—or to myself. How about you? What are you doing here on a Friday?" She nodded her chin at the notebook filled with his handwriting. "Paper?"

"Ten pages." He grinned. "To my girlfriend."

"Allison?" Julie asked. Then she blushed. "I overheard a phone call you were making the other day. I didn't mean to. Really." She wasn't in the habit of telling strangers that she'd noticed them, but this guy didn't feel like a stranger. Still, Julie knew she was turning red. She looked down at the table.

"Well, I might as well confess—I overheard you on the phone, too," he said. "Actually, I already knew about your jerk of a professor. And about Matt, too." Julie looked up again, and she and the guy laughed. His cheeks were pink also. "So much for privacy at college, huh? By the way, I'm Nicholas Stone."

"Julie. Julie Miller. Nice to meet you."

"Same," Nicholas said. "So, Julie Miller, where are you from?"

"Philadelphia," Julie said. "Matt's back there working. How about you?"

"Chappaqua," Nicholas said. "That's in Westchester County—north of New York City. Allison's from there, too, but she's in the city studying acting now."

Julie nodded. She knew that meant New York City. All the kids she'd met from New York referred to it as "the city," as if it were the only one in the world. "Are you an actor, too?"

Nicholas shook his head. "Nah. No way. I'm into archaeology and geology."

"Really? Cool," Julie said. Come to think of it, Nicholas looked a little like Harrison Ford in the Indiana Jones movies.

"Allison doesn't think it's so cool," Nicholas said. "She says she can't understand why I would want to dig up bone fragments with a toothbrush in some pit." He laughed. "I guess we're sort of a case of opposites attracting."

"Yeah, Matt and I are pretty different, too," Julie said. "But he's my best friend, really." She thought about the bouquet of roses he'd sent and smiled.

"How long have you been going out?" Nicholas asked, lowering his voice as the girl at the end of the table shot them another dirty look.

"Two years. What about you?"

"Wow. Allison and I just got together this summer. I mean, I've liked her for a lot longer than that, but . . . It's kind of a long story. Like about three years long. I guess you could say I was secretly in love with her for all that time." He paused a moment, looking at Julie. "Boring?"

Julie shook her head. "Not at all." *Pretty juicy, in fact,* she thought. She leaned back in her chair, ready for Nicholas's real-life love story.

"The bad part of the story is that she was going out with my best friend before we got together," Nicholas admitted.

Julie frowned. Nicholas didn't seem like someone who'd put the moves on his best friend's girlfriend.

"I know what you're thinking. You're going, 'What a sleaze bucket,'" Nicholas said. Julie wasn't sure what to answer. "Believe me, I'm not proud of it," he insisted. "Ben was the reason I never even let myself think for a second that anything could happen. But I couldn't help how I felt about Allison. Then, this summer, I came home from a dig in New Mexico while Ben was still away. I spent a lot of time hanging out at the restaurant where Allison was waiting tables. And then more time with her away from the restaurant. By the time Ben got back, it was too late. I mean, I just lose my head when it comes to Allison."

Nicholas sounded so sincere—and so in love.

Julie couldn't help softening. "I guess if it's meant to be, it's meant to be," she said.

Nicholas smiled. "Yeah. I feel like a pretty lucky guy." The smile turned into a frown. "Except it really messed things up between me and Ben. Can't blame the dude much, though."

"So where is he now?"

"He's in New York, too. Columbia. He and Allison wanted to be in the same city. That was before I got in the way. I don't think they're even talking right now."

"That's too bad," Julie said. It was funny how things worked out. She and Matt had never made a decision to stay in the same place, and yet she felt they were more in love than ever. Nicholas clearly felt the same way about Allison. "Well, I'll let you get back to your letter," she said. "If Allison's anything like me, she's probably already waiting at her mailbox for it."

Nicholas got a funny expression on his face. "You think?"

Julie was surprised. She couldn't imagine getting a letter from Matt and not ripping it open immediately and reading it a dozen times. Was it so different between Allison and Nicholas?

Down at the other end of the table, the girl who'd been shushing them slammed her book shut, gathered her things, and got up in a huff.

"Maybe you should forget those two back home and go have a date—away from me," she said.

As she stormed off to another table Julie and Nicholas shook their heads and laughed. "Did you notice she waited till the end of your story?" Julie said.

She knew she and Nicholas were going to be friends.

Ten

❧

Julie walked across Central Bowl on her way to the mail room. She wished she could feel happy after handing in her journalism assignment, but all she felt was a vague kind of relief.

She'd never thought that writing a three-paragraph article about an imaginary dead factory worker from Ohio would take so long. She'd spent the entire night in the library on Friday, and then half of Saturday and all of Sunday working on it. Julie had wanted it to be perfect, just like her papers and projects in high school. If there was one thing that was going to distinguish her from the other journalism students, it would be her dedication to her work.

But instead of feeling good about her accomplishment, Julie was simply relieved that it was finished. Maybe it was because she couldn't imagine being happy about anything that had to do with Professor Copeland's class. Or maybe it was because it was an obituary. Writing about that old man's death only made her think about Mary Beth.

Why couldn't Copeland have given them a birth announcement to write? Or a wedding announcement, or even a divorce announcement? Anything would have been more cheerful.

At least it's done, she thought as she pushed open the door to Walker Main's mail room. And maybe there would be something from home in her mailbox to pick up her spirits.

The mail room was so packed with students that Julie practically had to fight her way to the wall of identical rectangular boxes. She felt herself relax into a smile as she noticed through the tiny window in her box that there was mail for her. She quickly dialed her combination and pulled out not one but three letters, all from Philadelphia. Her parents, Tommy, and best of all, Matt. Monday was suddenly starting to look a lot less gloomy. She began to rip open the letter from Matt. Then she thought again and decided to save the best for last. Maybe she'd even wait until she got back to her room to read it.

She leaned against the wall of mailboxes and opened up Tommy's letter instead. An instant smile covered her face. On the first page was a cartoon drawing with the caption *Life at home: same as it ever was.* Tommy had sketched a picture of himself, frowning, in the middle, with his parents on either side. Her father, in his preacher's collar, was shaking a fist at Tommy, and her mother had a timid, helpless look on her face. In a thought balloon above Tommy's head was a little motorcycle; and her father was saying, "The eleventh commandment says, 'Thou shalt not purchase a trail bike with your allowance savings.'"

Julie hardly needed to read the letter to find out how Tommy was doing. It was no surprise that since she had gone off to college, her parents had become even more protective of Tommy. No trail bike, no overnight camping trip to the Poconos, and no hanging out at the mall after school. Not only that, but they were making him sing in the church choir, even though everybody in the congregation was fully aware that he was tone-deaf.

They're still real sad about Mary Beth. I am, too, Tommy had written. *But I don't see why I can't have a trail bike. Maybe you could write to them and tell them how bad I want it. I miss you a lot, Julie. It's lonely around here.*

Julie felt a lump in her throat. She wished she

could be there right at that moment. She'd gather him up in her arms and give him a super bear hug. Then she'd sneak him off to Matt's and let him ride on the back of Matt's Harley.

As expected, the letter from her folks got right to the point. No funny cartoons, just her mother's carefully penned script, which Julie knew so well. *Nice to hear from you, Julie. We can tell from your letter that you're doing well. It must be wonderful meeting new friends from all over the country. We're glad you're getting along with your room-mate. Your father and I don't think it was a great idea to let her buy you a new dress, however.*

Typical, Julie thought. As she finished the letter there was one line that stuck out: *Have you met any new boys? Anyone special?*

Julie wanted to tear the letter up. Why didn't they just come right out and say it? *We're really glad you and Matt are separated. Love, Mom and Dad.*

Well, I've got news for you, Mom and Dad. We're not separated. In fact, we're closer than ever! Julie couldn't believe that after two years, they were still so unwilling to accept Matt as a part of her life. And still so unwilling to accept the hard and cold truth about Mary Beth's death—that it wasn't Matt's fault that she'd died—or even Matt's father's fault. It was her own fault for getting into that car when she was drunk, for letting herself get so out of control.

Enough! Julie told herself. Her hand, holding all her letters, was trembling. But she knew there was one surefire way to cheer herself up. Instead of waiting until she got back to the dorm, she opened Matt's letter immediately. As she slid the pages from the envelope she wished that her parents could have seen the bouquet of roses she had gotten from him—one flower for every kiss she'd love to give to him right in front of her mother and father.

She got as far as *Dear Julie* before she felt herself shoved aside. "Excuse me," a tall, skinny guy with a nasal voice said sarcastically. "Maybe you could you give me some idea of when you're gonna finish reading, so I can get to my box. I've got class in an hour."

"I didn't know it was a crime to read letters," Julie snapped back. Impulsively she stuck her tongue out at the boy, then walked away. "And I hope your box is empty," she said as she headed off.

She read Matt's letter as she walked down the hallway toward the snack bar, not caring that she was bumping into people and making them walk around her.

He'd enclosed pictures of him and Steven in

the Poconos. In one, they stood at the summit of Mount Airy, with Steven holding a sign with an arrow pointing to Matt. *He misses you, Julie,* the sign read.

So much for Matt and me being separated, she thought with a smile.

"Julie, over here," a voice called out. It was Dahlia, sitting at a booth in the rear of the snack bar with blond, suntanned Andy, who definitely looked the part of Mr. College Swim Team. With them were a couple of guys Julie didn't know. *Leave it to Dahlia,* she thought. Julie figured that Dahlia would know pretty much the entire campus by next Tuesday. A little hesitant, Julie walked over and joined them.

"Look," Julie said, showing Dahlia the picture of Matt and Steven. "Isn't he the cutest?"

"Put that away, girl," Dahlia said, ignoring the photo. "Sit down and meet my friends Michael and Max. They're in my English class. Guys, this is Julie, my roommate. She's from Philadelphia."

Julie said hello, but she barely heard the rest of the conversation. She slumped down in the booth and continued reading the letter from Matt. She blushed every time the word *love* appeared, and she tried to cover the letter from view.

"Don't mind her," Dahlia said, "she's still lost

in boyfriend-back-home land. Maybe one of you guys can help her find her way out."

"Doesn't look like it," Max said. "Look at the smile on her face. Lucky girl."

"Hey, Julie, how many days till Thanksgiving?" Dahlia asked with a touch of sarcasm.

Julie looked up from the letter. "Sixty-two. You can tease me all you want, but I don't care. I'm in love. And so's Matt." But just for Dahlia's sake, she folded up the letter and put it in her bag.

"That's better," Dahlia said. "I'm sure Matt's a great guy and all, but, hey, join the club for a little while."

"Yeah, I'll get you a cup of coffee," Michael said.

Julie laughed. "Okay, thanks. With lots of milk, if you don't mind."

But as she hung out in the snack bar and listened to stories about how Max's roommate snored and how Michael had lived in San Diego for sixteen years, she couldn't help thinking that the Madison social life was for single people, like Dahlia. She was in her element with Andy—her boyfriend of the moment—on one side of her, funny-looking Max with the big head on the other, and Michael sitting across from her. The funniest thing of all was that meanwhile, Dahlia was busy dreaming about Sarah's brother, Tim.

118

And who knew whom she would meet the next day?

Madison was for people like Marion, too. She'd come there in search of her "perfect specimen," as she called it. Fresh off the farm, Marion was looking for Mr. Right first and a college education second. Same with Sarah Pike, same with Paul Chase, same with Andy, same with Max and Michael. They were all looking for love—some for a night or two, some forever.

But Julie *was* in love. She'd already found her Mr. Right. Sitting there with everyone, nodding her head and saying "uh-huh" and "really?" she felt as if she was only pretending to be part of the crowd.

Oh my gosh! There he is! Marion knew Fred was nearby practically before she took a look. It was as if sirens were going off in her head to signal his presence. She turned around, and there he was, walking across the green stretch of Central Bowl toward the library. Squinting into the bright sun, all Marion could see from her vantage point was his reddish hair and his bouncy walk, but Marion knew immediately who it was.

She wanted to race toward him, but she found herself frozen to the lawn. He'd been so easy to talk to in bio lab, but all of a sudden she was sure she'd be tongue-tied. *Come on,* she told herself. *You're gonna miss your chance.* Fred passed the side entrance to Walker Main and was getting closer to the sweeping, curved walls and glinting windows of the library.

Marion tried to imagine what someone like Dahlia would say to Fred. She sure knew how to talk to boys. Marion pictured herself sauntering up to Fred and tossing her hair the way she'd seen Dahlia do. *Hi, Fred. Going off to study on such a beautiful day?* she'd say. *Oh, wow, but it's so nice out. Maybe we should just hang out at the quarry or something. Go for a swim.* Marion took a few steps. She stopped again. No way. She'd never say that to a boy in a million years.

Well, what would Julie say, then? She had a boyfriend—a real, steady, long-term boyfriend. She'd know just how to talk to Fred. She'd probably walk right up to him as if it was the most natural thing in the world. *Hey, Fred!* she'd say in a friendly, casual way. *Going to do your bio homework? Great. Maybe we can work on it together.*

Marion practiced that opening line as she started toward Fred again. "Hey, Fred!" she said softly. "Going to do your bio homework?" And what if he wasn't? What if he said he was going to the library to study ancient Greek?

Then maybe there was Susan's approach.

Susan would probably smile shyly and say what a lovely day it was. Then she'd stand there serenely and be so sweet that Fred would just melt. But Marion knew she couldn't come face-to-face with Fred and be anything but jittery and full of butterflies. Still, her feet were carrying her toward him.

Fred started up the long, gently inclined ramp to the library entrance. She sped up until she was almost behind him. "Fred!" she called out. Her voice sounded too loud and too urgent. What if he didn't even know who she was outside of class?

But he turned around, and she could see him smile. He waited for her as she hurried to meet him. She felt as if everyone around them must be able to hear her heart beating. "Uh, hi!" she said awkwardly. There were those eyes—chocolate with flecks of gold. "Marion. Remember?"

"Sure I do. Hi, Marion. How're you doing?" he asked.

"Good. And you?" Well, it wasn't exactly the way Dahlia would play it, but at least she'd gotten a couple of words out. After the formalities—"I'm fine. Nice day, isn't it?"—there was a long pause.

Marion shifted from one sneaker to the other. "Um, I'm looking forward to the next bio lab," she finally managed, the beginning of the sentence coming out in a squeak. *Great. That was a really interesting thing to say.*

But Fred bobbed his head in agreement. "Me, too. I've never dissected a crayfish before."

"Me either. I wonder if it's like eating a lobster —you know, you do the claws and everything first, and save the tail for last," Marion said.

"Do crayfish have claws?" Fred asked.

"Actually, I have no idea," Marion said. She couldn't believe she was standing there talking to Fred without pretending she was Dahlia or Julie or Susan. She was just being herself, and Fred seemed to think that was fine.

"Well, um, maybe we could do a little studying and find out," Fred said. "Do some prep work for the next lab—if you've got the time."

Marion smiled into Fred's brown eyes. "I've got my bio book right in my bag."

It was that awful part of the phone call again.

Julie had told Matt all about her classes. Human Biology was absolutely fascinating, and did he know that people were ninety-five percent water? Literature was her best subject, as usual. Her French teacher had given the class so many recipes that Julie thought she must harbor a secret fantasy about becoming a chef, and journalism— well, she'd rather not even think about that. She'd told him how Dahlia was dating Andy but dreaming about Tim. She'd filled him in on every detail about her schoolwork, her job in the cafeteria, and everyone on her hall.

Matt had told Julie about work at the club, and how he was trying to save enough money to move into his own place. "Living with Dad and Suzanna really makes me feel like a kid," he'd said. He'd told her about how he and Steven had gotten caught in a thunderstorm on their most recent rock-climbing trip, and that he'd run into Tommy and a friend at Mr. Pizza.

They'd reminisced about the summer and talked about what they were going to do over Thanksgiving. They'd told each other a few jokes and made dumb noises into the telephone. But now Julie felt the tension of their imminent goodbye. If only they could say, "See you tomorrow." If only the kisses they blew through the phone could be real.

"Hey, Matt, remember when you said we should just run off and get married?" she joked. "Is the offer still good?"

Matt's tenor laugh came through the phone. "Man, maybe I oughta just hop on my bike and come out for a little visit this weekend."

"Yeah, that would be great." Julie sighed. "Except that I'm going to be spending the whole weekend in the library."

"So? I'll go hiking while you're studying," Matt said.

"Hiking? In Ohio? And what would you do for exercise?" Julie looked out the dorm window at the bare cornfields, which stretched level for as far as she could see. She laughed. "Matt, sweetie, the biggest hill in the vicinity is Mount Landfill, behind the football field. They built it when they dug the foundation for the new gym so the cross-country track team would have something to practice on."

Matt whistled through his teeth. "That flat out there, huh? Well, I could just tool around on my bike and check things out, I guess."

Julie heard Matt's tone go from wishing to suggesting. "Hey, you're serious, aren't you?" She had a flash of Matt sitting next to her—right there, on her bed—and of hanging out with him on the grass of Central Bowl, of introducing him to Dahlia and all her new friends. Then she glanced over at the stack of books on her desk and her little computer, which was switched on, the cursor blinking at her—a green flash of conscience. "The thing is, I've got a ton of work to do. And you have to work at the Fast Lane, anyway. Weekends are the busiest."

"I could get a few days off. Don't you want me to come out?" Matt asked softly.

Julie felt a cramp of hurt. "Of course I want you to, but I just don't think it's a good idea." If Matt came out, there was no way she was going to sit in the library and study. "I mean, I'm at school for a reason, right? And if I'm not going to get my work done, I might as well be back in Philly."

There was a chilly silence at the other end. Then, "Julie, we're talking a weekend here. One weekend. I thought you wanted to see me as much as I want to see you," Matt said.

"I do." Julie's hand was tight around the phone receiver.

"But what, Julie?"

Julie looked at her computer and her schoolbooks. Matt was right. It was one weekend. Then why did she have such a nervous feeling in the pit of her stomach? "I don't know, Matt. I guess I'm afraid that if you come out here, I'm gonna start thinking I never should have gone away in the first place."

"Well, maybe you shouldn't have."

"Listen, I made a plan and I'm just trying to give it a chance, okay?" Julie heard her voice come out tight and defensive. She was trying hard to stay on course. Why was Matt working against her?

"Ah, the Julie plan. Right," Matt said, his words clipped.

Julie felt a tickle of annoyance. "You know, Matt, some people believe in making plans."

"Well, some people are so damn busy making plans that they miss out on life completely," Matt threw back.

His words felt like a slap in the face. "Whoa!" Julie said, taking a few deep breaths. "That's kind of harsh, don't you think? I mean, maybe if my sister had done a little more planning and a little less playing . . ." Her words trailed off.

Matt sighed deeply at the other end. "I'm sorry, Jules," he finally said. "Really, I am. I guess I just miss you too much. Look, why are we fighting?"

"I don't know." Julie sank onto her bed. "I just think that if we go running to Philadelphia or Ohio whenever we really miss each other, we're never going to make it through four years apart. I feel like I'm on the outside of college life enough already."

"Jules, sometimes you're so damned practical," Matt said.

Julie felt her throat constrict. "Look, maybe we

126

should just get off the phone, okay? We'll try again fresh next time."

"Like I said, practical. Well . . . okay." There was a brief silence. "I'll—talk to you. Bye."

"Bye," Julie whispered. She didn't make a move to hang up. God, this was awful. How could she get off the phone when things were so unsettled? When the distance between them felt like a wall?

"Jules?" Matt's voice was thick. "Julie, you know I love you," he said. "I don't want to fight."

Julie felt one tear roll down her cheek. "Me either. I love you, too, Matt."

"Okay, see you," Matt said.

"Yeah, see you," Julie echoed.

She heard the hard, final click on his end, then the hollow sound of the line going dead. She got up and put the receiver back in its cradle. The tears came faster and harder. She wanted to call Matt back immediately and make everything all right. Maybe she should have let him come out to visit. So what if she didn't get all her work done? What difference would a missed assignment make if she were in Matt's arms? *Go on, Julie. Be impulsive for once,* she told herself. *Go for it.*

She wiped her eyes with the hem of her T-shirt and stared at the telephone. Then she looked toward her computer. The cursor blinked steadily. She felt her resolve returning.

No. No, she couldn't give up. She got up and went to her desk. She had four whole years without Matt ahead of her and she had to get used to it. It was an awfully long time. She couldn't even think of giving up now, or she would be gone.

Eleven

❧

Sheltered by her oversized red umbrella, Dahlia slid into the bleachers just in time to see Tim zigzagging his way across the football field. He hugged the ball close to him, like it was a cache of precious goods. From every direction on the muddy field, players rushed toward him, huge in their pads and helmets. Tim dodged one way and then another, picking his way through the moving obstacle course.

"Watch out!" Dahlia found herself yelling as an oversized player ran up behind him and lunged. Suddenly, a half-dozen guys were on top of him, bringing him crashing to the ground at the bottom of a big heap. But as the pile of bodies fell away from one another, Tim emerged, football in hand, and stood up. He was sopping wet, and his uniform with the purple number fifteen on it was covered with mud.

Dahlia let out a breath of relief and looked around her. Except for one couple, way up at the top of the bleachers, the stadium was empty, the rain keeping any other fans away. What a miserable day to be out there chasing after some weird-shaped ball in the mud. Dahlia looked at her watch. According to her sources—the jocks on the next hall—football practice was just about over. She'd gotten there at exactly the right time.

She watched Tim throw the ball to a teammate in the middle of the field. The guy caught it and started running toward Tim and the others. He tried to race past the gang of purple-and-white gorillas, but they jumped on top of him and brought him down.

Dahlia tapped one foot impatiently. She didn't really understand the thrill of these boys' games. She had other things in mind when it came to physical activity. Finally, after a few more pileups, an older man in a pair of purple Madison College sweats came running out onto the field, blowing his whistle. "That's it, guys," she heard him yell. "Postmortem in the locker room in five minutes."

Dahlia stood up as the players ran around high-fiving one another and slapping one another on the back. She picked out number fifteen again, and when Tim came off the field, she intercepted him. "Hey, Tim!" she said, raising her umbrella to let him under.

"Oh, hi!" Tim grinned. "Dahlia, from my sister's hall, right? I wondered who the diehard fan was, coming out in the rain."

"Yeah, I didn't see much, though," Dahlia said, sheltering him with her umbrella so that her arm was almost resting on his big padded shoulder. "Did you make a lot of touchdowns?"

Tim smiled. "Yeah, a couple."

Two of his teammates walked by and laughed. "Looks like Pike's gonna score again," one of them said.

"Hot car, too," she heard the other one say as they headed for the back door of the gym.

Tim leaned in even closer. "Looks like you and your convertible are turning some heads around here," he said. "Even if you don't know anything about football."

Dahlia felt herself blushing. "Well, that's why I'm here. I thought maybe you could teach me a thing or two." With her free hand, she touched him lightly on the arm. She could feel his muscles through the wet fabric of his uniform.

"About football?" Tim arched an eyebrow over his blue-green eyes.

"Whatever," Dahlia tossed back. "I thought

131

maybe you'd want to grab a bite to eat, if you're not doing anything. We could drive over to the Barn and Grill."

"My number-one hangout. Jake—he and his wife, Patricia, own the place—used to play for Madison. Great burgers."

"Does that mean yes?" Dahlia asked.

Tim hesitated. "You know I have a steady girlfriend."

Dahlia shrugged. "Yeah? I'm sort of seeing someone, too," she said.

Tim looked into Dahlia's eyes. His face was close to hers, and he smelled of mud and rain. "Well, if that doesn't bother you, sure, I'd love to hang out for a while."

Dahlia smiled up at him. "Great." Girlfriend? Maybe. Steady? She'd see about that.

"Well, the coach wants to talk to us, and I've gotta take a shower. Meet you out in front of the gym in twenty minutes?"

"I'll be waiting," Dahlia said.

This was one game that she knew how to play.

Julie whacked the alarm with the palm of her hand and groaned. Why now, when she was dreaming about Matt? She couldn't quite remember the dream, but they'd been up at the top of some mountain somewhere—which definitely left out Madison as a possible location. Julie buried herself deeper under the covers and tried to recall the dream. Maybe she'd just go back to sleep. Forget about—

Journalism! She was suddenly awake. Copeland was going to return the obituaries that day. Her dream faded in the light streaming in through her window. She sat up in bed. *Please let me do well,* she thought. *Please.*

She pushed off the covers and swung her feet over the side of the bed, feeling around for her slippers. Then she tiptoed over to the door to Dahlia's side of the room and put her hand on the knob.

A giggle from the other side of the door stopped her cold. "Good morning, good-looking," she heard Dahlia say through the paper-thin wall that divided their rooms.

Oh, no! Julie remembered waking up sometime in the middle of the night to the rhythmic squeaking of Dahlia's bedsprings and Dahlia and Andy's throaty sounds of pleasure. But the last time Andy had stayed over, he'd been gone by the time Julie had to wake up for class. Now she took a step away from the door. She was trapped. All her clothes were on Dahlia's side of the room —not to mention that the door to the hall was over there, too. Well, Julie was simply going to have to knock and let them know she was coming through.

"Dahlia? Damn, am I in trouble," said a deep voice. Julie felt her breath catch. That wasn't Andy's voice, was it? "I can't believe we fell asleep." No, it wasn't Andy at all.

Julie sank back down on her bed. "Shh!" she heard Dahlia saying. "Just come here, sexy. If you're in big trouble, there's nothing you can do about it. So why don't you come back to bed and worry about that later?"

Julie felt a burst of disbelief. Was Andy history already? What had it been? A couple of weeks? Now whom was Dahlia with? "Mmm, that's better," she heard Dahlia say. Then there came the sounds of soft, moist kisses and the movement of bodies under the sheets. The bed groaned and squeaked. Julie grumbled to herself. How was she supposed to go banging on the door when Dahlia was hot and heavy with some strange guy?

"Oh, Tim!" she heard Dahlia whisper.

Tim? Julie felt a jolt of anger. She knew Dahlia had her eye on Tim Pike, but she also knew that he had a serious girlfriend—one he was living with. Didn't that mean anything to either Dahlia or Tim? Didn't they care that someone else's feelings were involved? Julie thought about how Tim's sister was right down the hall. Wasn't it kind of flaunting it to do this right under her nose?

Julie let out a long breath. She knew it wasn't just Dahlia and Tim that had her so upset. As the sounds grew louder in the next room she thought about Matt's stinging words during that awful last phone conversation. *Some people are so damn busy making plans that they miss out on life completely.* What had Matt meant by that? Was he capable of doing to her what Tim was doing to his girlfriend? What Tim and Dahlia were doing to her? Julie didn't think so, but she didn't know for sure. There were always plenty of girls around the Fast Lane. And they weren't asking Matt to wait for them until Thanksgiving.

Julie realized her fists were clenched and she made an effort to relax. She took a few long breaths and opened her hands. She was simply going to have to trust Matt. She had no other choice. Meanwhile, she had a more concrete problem. Hard, fast breathing and cries of passion penetrated the wall. Julie was a prisoner.

She thought about Professor Copeland pacing in front of the class with the stack of obituaries. "Ms. Miller?" he'd say, searching the classroom for her.

What was she going to do? She looked out the window. People were walking by, starting the

135

day. The window! That was the solution. It was small—maybe half the size of her bedroom windows at home. But it led onto level, grassy ground. If she opened it all the way . . .

Julie got up and went over to take a closer look. Yes, she could squeeze out if she really had to. And she had to. She pulled on the oversized 76ers T-shirt she'd thrown on the floor next to her bed the night before. Then she pushed the bottom window all the way up.

As she climbed out, her book bag dangling from one arm, she was struck with the chill of the late-September morning. Her slippered feet hit the soft ground under her window, and she shivered. She hoped Marion or someone else on her hall could come through with something to wear, or Mr. Copeland was really going to have something to ridicule her about.

Twelve

❧

Matt rode his motorcycle down Auger Street. The early morning air was bracing against his face, the engine hummed in his ears. As he neared Julie's tidy yellow house he played a little game in his mind. What if Julie hadn't gone away to school? What if they hadn't ever had that dumb fight on the phone? What if nothing had changed? What if she were right at home, just waiting for him to come by and carry her off somewhere on his bike?

Auger Street was a rather out-of-the-way route to take to Steven's, but Matt couldn't resist a few minutes of this little fantasy. He imagined Julie sitting on her lawn reading the newspaper, looking up as the sound of his bike announced his arrival. He could almost see her long legs stretched out under the cherry tree in front of the house.

The neatly trimmed lawn came into view, the roof of the house rising into his vision. Then the branches of the cherry tree—and yes! There was someone under the tree! Matt immediately slowed down. "Yo! Tommy, my man!" he called out, stopping at the beginning of the Millers' driveway.

Tommy jumped up and ran over. With his thick dark hair and lean, long build, he looked a lot like Julie. "Matt!" he said happily, holding his hand out for a high five.

"Long time, bro. Aren't you supposed to be in school today?"

"Day off," Tommy informed him. "Parent-teacher meetings."

"So you decided to spend the morning hanging around under the cherry tree?" Matt said.

Tommy shrugged. "I was just thinking," he said noncommittally.

"Yeah? What about?" Matt asked, giving him a fake punch in the arm.

"Oh, stuff. How to get my folks to let me buy a dirt bike, mostly." Tommy eyed Matt's Harley hungrily.

Matt followed his gaze. "Well, I don't think I've

got an answer for that one, but I can give you a ride around the block if you want."

Tommy frowned and looked toward the house. "I wish," he said longingly. "But there's a problem. And here he comes." The Millers' front door opened, and Julie's father appeared in the doorway.

Matt felt a twinge of nervousness. He always did around Julie's parents. "Morning, sir!" he called out, raising his hand in a wave.

"Morning," Reverend Miller said stiffly, crossing the lawn and shaking Matt's hand—a brief, staccato motion without any warmth. "So, what brings you to visit, Matthew?"

Matt bristled at the use of his full name, as if the casualness of Matt were too common—not good enough. "I was just riding by," he said tightly. "And I saw Tommy, so I stopped to say hi."

"Oh, I see. Well. We just got a letter from Julie, and she sounds like she's having a really grand time at school—meeting all sorts of new people."

Grand? *Well, la-di-dah*, Matt wanted to say. Instead, he managed a frozen smile. "I sure hope she's having fun." He didn't comment on the meeting-new-people part, but he felt hollow in the pit of his stomach. He didn't need to hear this.

He stood uncomfortably, the conversation

stalled out before it had even gotten going. Tommy fidgeted nervously, too. "I guess I'd better be going," Matt finally said. "Tell Mrs. Miller I said hello." *Like I'm sure she cares,* he thought. "See you, sport!" He ruffled Tommy's hair.

"Bye, Matt," Tommy said. "Stop by again, okay?"

"Good-bye, Matthew," Reverend Miller said coldly.

"Good-bye, sir." Matt crossed the lawn and threw his leg over his bike. He revved the engine loudly. As he peeled away from Julie's house her father's words echoed in his head. *A grand time. New people. All sorts of new people.* He pushed the Harley to too high a speed for the quiet suburban streets, trying to drive out the hopelessness that was igniting inside him.

So much for his little fantasy game where nothing had changed. Julie was far away—and probably having new experiences every day. Matt wondered if her father's words were ugly because they were all too true. Was that why she didn't want him to come out and visit? Because she was having the time of her life without him?

Or did she miss him as much as he missed her? Was she as lonely? But the thought of Julie pining away for him was no comfort, either. Matt wanted her to be happy, and maybe he was

140

holding her back. Maybe the memory of them together was holding her back.

Matt took the next turn too quickly, his bike almost skidding out from under him. He didn't know which was worse—that Julie might be having the time of her life, or that she might not be.

College is supposed to be about new experiences, but this one's a little much, Julie thought as she crossed North Quad in Marion's clothes. Still, she felt pretty in a sort of old-fashioned way in Marion's green-and-white gingham dress, belted at the waist, a pair of tennis shoes—a little too large—and white anklet socks. The dress looked as if it might have come from someone's grandmother's attic, but Julie had tried to do herself up the way Dahlia might have under the circumstances—retro, with red lipstick to complete the look. Marion's roommate, Susan, too tiny to have been of much help with the clothes, had come through with a lip gloss that she used when she played a concert—a fire-engine red bright enough to stand out onstage.

Julie crossed the street and headed toward Fischer. *If Matt could see me now,* she thought. *Or while I was climbing out the window in my T-shirt.* Well, she'd have a good story to tell next time she wrote to him. She sighed. Maybe she and Dahlia shouldn't wait till the middle of the year to switch rooms. After all, how much privacy did she need to carry on a relationship by mail and telephone? It certainly would make it more convenient when she needed to get to class in the morning.

She pushed open the glass doors of Fischer and followed the crowd going up the stairs. She hoped it was worth all the hassle she'd gone through to get there. *Please let me get an A,* she thought as she entered Professor Copeland's classroom.

"Hi," she said to the guy with the long red-blond hair, slipping into the seat next to him. She didn't know his first name yet because Professor Copeland called him Mr. Graham. "That's quite a mane, Mr. Graham," he'd commented the week before. "What is the statement you're trying to make?"

Now Mr. Graham arched a surprised eyebrow at Julie. "Wow, I'm impressed. I didn't think I'd see you again after the way the guy was dumping on you," he said.

Julie raised her shoulders. "I'm not going to let him scare me into dropping his class. I guess he's just trying to make us into hard-boiled journalists." She was acting far more confident than she really was. Waiting for Professor Copeland to hand back the assignment was a little like waiting for her SAT scores to come back. While she might seem collected on the outside, on the inside she was a nervous wreck.

She felt her whole body tense up as Professor Copeland entered with a flourish, a stack of papers in his hands. He dropped the papers on his desk, grabbed a piece of chalk from the ledge under the blackboard, and began scribbling furiously. *Objective journalism,* he wrote in a bold but ragged hand.

He threw the chalk back down and jabbed at the word with his finger. "How many people think this is the bottom line for any good newspaperman—or -woman?" he added with an exaggerated nod in Julie's direction.

Julie wanted to melt under her desk. Why couldn't he cut her some slack, just for one day? But she made herself keep her gaze level and trained on Professor Copeland. Around her, no one made a move to raise his or her hand.

"Nobody?" Professor Copeland thundered. He gave the blackboard a loud rap with his knuckles. "No one in this room believes in objective journalism?"

Julie found herself trying to figure out what his little trick was this time. Were they supposed to say yes or no? She felt a flitter of disgust—more at herself than at Professor Copeland. Of

143

course she believed in objective journalism. That was what she'd spent the weekend in the library trying to achieve—a fair, concise, accurate portrayal of the man who had died. She put her hand up in the air.

"Ah, Ms. Miller. Well, I'm glad to see someone had the courage to take a stand." Julie allowed herself a small smile. It was the first glimmer of praise she'd gotten from her professor. "Anyone else?" he asked, his gaze ricocheting from one student to the next. "Objective journalism, anyone?"

A few more students raised their hands. Then some others. "Yes, I see," Professor Copeland said. "And it shows in the assignments you turned in."

Wow, did we do something right for a change? Julie wondered.

"Now, I'd like one of you to tell me why objective journalism is so important," Professor Copeland challenged, his eyes searching out his victim.

Before he'd picked a target, Julie found herself speaking up. "We have a responsibility to provide the readers with the facts," she said, "so they can form their own opinions."

"Is that so?" Professor Copeland asked. He picked up the chalk again and slashed the words he'd written on the blackboard with a big X. "Wrong!" he announced with authority. Julie felt her heart sink.

"Do you really think objective journalism sells newspapers?" Professor Copeland asked, planting himself in front of the class with his arms folded. "Which would you rather pay for? Dry, antiseptic facts, or guts and drama and excitement? Do you think John Q. Public would rather watch the news reporter who calmly announces an aviation accident or the reporter who talks about the tragedy and the destruction, the scores of dead, the twisted, charred wreckage of the airplane, and the grief-stricken faces of the relatives?"

Julie grimaced with distaste. "Professor Copeland, are you saying that you advocate sensationalist journalism?" Maybe she was in the wrong class after all. Maybe she should be looking for a professor who had some scruples and some dignity.

Professor Copeland rubbed the top of his shiny head. "Ms. Miller, I want you to take a moment and think before you answer. Think honestly, find the truth. One television station makes an unemotional, straightforward announcement about a plane crash—cause of the accident, death toll, where the injured are being taken. Period.

End of story. Now the other station describes it graphically. It shows you the horrific footage of the wrecked, burned plane. It broadcasts the sirens and the cries of despair, gives you interviews with the survivors. Which station do you turn to? Honestly, Ms. Miller."

Julie slumped in her chair. She didn't even need a moment to think about the answer. She wanted to say that she'd tune in to the station that reported the facts, that didn't resort to selling human tragedy. But it wasn't true. Maybe it was only human to be curious about the gory details. "The second station," she mumbled unhappily.

"Of course you'd watch the second station!" Professor Copeland said. "Because the truth is not simple facts. The truth is deeper than that. The truth is what you feel. What the public feels."

He took the stack of papers from his desk and began passing them out. "Flannery, Gilchrist, Graham . . ." There were groans all around the room as people got their obituaries back. Julie didn't hold any hope for herself. After that little lesson, what could she expect? C? C-plus? She'd never gotten anything less than a B in high school. *But hey, college is a time for new experiences,* she thought gloomily. She wiggled her feet nervously in Marion's overly roomy sneakers.

"Miller," Professor Copeland said, tapping her

paper down on her desk, blank side up. She prepared herself and turned it over. F! The ugly red letter screamed at her from the top of the page. F? No way. F, as in failure, flunked, forget it? She might not have turned the death of an old factory worker into the major news item of the month, but she had gotten all the facts down, and her article was clear and well written. Didn't that count for anything? She thought about how Professor Copeland didn't believe in being objective. Maybe he didn't believe in being fair, either.

She looked back down at her paper. *No drama,* Professor Copeland had written. *Where's the human-interest element?* The guy was eighty-six years old. He'd died in his sleep. He'd spent his life making machine parts. How dramatic could a person be about that?

Julie felt flushed with frustration and anger. Who did this guy think he was? She shot him a hateful glare as he finished handing back the papers and took his position in front of the class.

"Now, I know most of you will be unhappy with your grades," he said mildly, stroking his beard like a cat preening. "You may have worked hard on this little assignment. You may have done a perfectly nice job with the writing." The cat sprang. "But journalism is a business, people!" he yelled. "Either it sells, or it doesn't.

There is no such thing as a C-minus in this business—so I don't give them out in my class. Now, if you'll put your papers away," he went on, the mild manner returning, "I'd like to begin today's lesson."

Julie folded her work so that the red F was hidden from view. But her fingers trembled as she tucked the sheet into her book bag. For this she had climbed out of her window half dressed? For this she had worked all weekend long? For this she had left Matt four hundred miles away?

She found herself wishing she'd never left Philadelphia.

"What do you mean, did I do my best?" Julie yelled into the telephone. "Do you think I purposely tried to get an F? Like it's some new experience I wanted to try?" What a mistake it had been to think that her mother and father would cheer her up.

"Young lady, it's not going to help to get sarcastic," her father said sharply. "Your mother was simply asking a question."

"Yes, I tried my hardest, even if you don't believe me," Julie shot back. "You know, I called you because I thought it might make me feel better. Not worse."

"Sweetheart," her mother began, "no one's

trying to make you feel worse. I promise. I just wanted to make sure that there isn't anything bothering you. Something that might be getting in the way of your work."

Her mother's tone was far calmer than her father's, but Julie felt herself instantly grow more tense. "Something? For example?" She remembered her parents' last letter, the one in which her mother had not so subtly told Julie to forget about Matt.

"Well . . . anything. Making new friends, being away from home, meeting boys . . ."

Julie felt a wave of anger overtake her. "For your information, I'm not trying to meet boys." Her loud voice echoed off the walls of her little dorm room.

She heard her mother sigh into the receiver. "That was what I was afraid of," she said.

"You know, Julie, it's a wonderful time in your life," her father sermonized. "Learning new things, opening up to new ideas, new people, new relationships." Julie gritted her teeth as her father went on. "You don't want to wake up one day and realize you've missed out on that."

Save it for Sunday morning services, she thought. "What happened to make new friends but keep the old?" she asked, her voice shaking. "What about that part of your little speech?"

"Julie, darling, your father and I want you to be happy. Believe us," her mother said.

"Mom, Matt makes me happy," Julie shouted. "Why can't *you* believe *me*?"

"I know it's hard for you to imagine it right now, but there will be other boys," her mother argued. "Boys you care for just as much. More. It's normal, what you're going through. Everyone has a first love. A puppy love."

"Puppy love! Is that what you think it is?" Julie was on her feet now, pacing the room with hard, furious steps.

"Julie, sweetie, calm down," her mother implored. "I know you care very deeply for Matt, but he's not the only boy in the world. I'm simply saying you should be open to new possibilities."

"Look, think what you want," Julie said flatly. "I know how I feel about Matt and I know it's real." There was a long silence on the line. "Is Tommy around?" Julie finally said stiffly. "I'd like to talk to him."

"Julie," her mother said quietly, "just think about what we've said."

"I don't see how I can help it," Julie answered. She waited for Tommy to come to the phone. At least one person in her family supported her.

Thirteen

❧

"Okay, Julie, you've made your point," Dahlia yelled from the other half of the room. "You woke up on the wrong side of the bed. But I don't think it's very fair to take it out on me."

Julie sat at her desk, her journalism assignment with the red F in front of her. "What wrong side?" she yelled back. "The only side I could get out on today was the window side." She felt the tears welling up in her eyes. If Madison was going to be about firsts like this, she didn't want any part of it. Her first bad phone call with Matt. Her first failing grade. Her first long-distance fight with her parents. And now her first fight with Dahlia, too.

"I just can't believe you'd go and break up a serious relationship, Dahlia!"

"Me?" Dahlia's voice was angry. Julie heard

her get up off her bed and cross her room, picking her way through some boxes that she still hadn't unpacked. "It takes two, Julie," she said from the doorway between their two sides. "I mean, I didn't force the guy to do anything he didn't want to do. Believe me. Besides, who said anything about breaking them up?"

Julie pushed her chair back, the legs squeaking against the tile floor. "Oh, come on, Dahlia. You mean you don't care that Tim has a girlfriend?"

Dahlia shrugged. "Well, maybe a little. I mean, I really like him, I think."

"And what about Andy?"

Dahlia shrugged again. "I don't know. I like him, too."

Julie let out a loud breath between her teeth. "The more the merrier? Dahlia, it just doesn't work that way." She felt like telling Dahlia to grow up a little.

Dahlia plunked down on Julie's patchwork bedspread. "And you know how it does work?" she asked tightly. "Like maybe you spend all your time staring at a few pictures and talking on the telephone with someone you've left four hundred miles away?"

Julie winced. "Thanks, Dahlia. That makes me feel really great," she said. "Whose side are you on? My parents'?" The tears threatened to spill again, and she blinked hard and fast.

"Well, how do you think you're making me feel?" Dahlia asked. "Like I'm some kind of criminal for hanging out with a guy I really like. Not everyone is the same as you and Matt, you know. Maybe Tim's relationship with his girlfriend isn't that great. Maybe he actually wants to break up with her. Did you ever think of that? Or maybe they have some agreement that it's okay to see other people. Not every couple acts like they're married. Can't you see anything but how it is for you?"

Julie felt chastened. Was she really being so self-involved? She bit her lip. "To tell you the truth," she said quietly, "I don't feel like my relationship with Matt is so great these days."

Dahlia's anger seemed to deflate into an expression of pain. "Hey, come on, Julie. I didn't mean it that way," she said. "I just want you to look at it from my point of view. But I know you and Matt have something special going."

"Had," Julie said. "This week, all we have is a couple of letters from each other and a lousy phone call."

"And a dozen incredible roses."

"Almost dead." Julie heard how melodramatic her words sounded, and she couldn't help laugh-

153

ing a little. She really was acting awfully sorry for herself.

"That's better," Dahlia said. "Look, let's not be mad at each other, okay?"

"Okay," Julie agreed.

"And next time I have company, go ahead and knock on the door. We can deal."

Julie rolled her eyes. "Listen, what if we switched rooms right away, Dahlia?"

Dahlia's forehead creased. "What? After I've just about unpacked everything and decided where to put it? I don't know. Lemme think about it."

"Sure," Julie said.

"So, what are we doing tonight?" Dahlia asked, putting the fight behind them. Julie still didn't feel very good about Dahlia and Tim, but she knew she needed a friend more than a fight just then.

"Big party at Old Wilder," Dahlia went on. Old Wilder was a dorm on the other side of campus.

Julie raised her shoulders. "I don't know. I was planning to stay home and do some work. I've gotta have the first half of *La Maison de Claudine* finished by the end of next week for French."

"*La* what?" Dahlia asked. "Come on, Julie. You spent last Friday night studying, too. You gotta have some fun, babe."

154

Julie sighed. "I suppose. But I did want to try and talk to Matt tonight. I've been calling and he's not home, so I thought I'd get him at work later."

"And you're going to stay home just to make one phone call?" Dahlia asked. She shook her head, as if Julie were a lost cause.

Julie tried to explain. "Dahlia, I really want to straighten things out with him. Besides, I think he'd make me feel better about this F. My folks sure didn't."

"You'll live," Dahlia said. "I've gotten lots of F's. Every time I get one I buy myself a new dress."

"Is that how you got such a big wardrobe?" Julie joked. In a funny way, she was impressed by Dahlia's attitude. But Julie knew she could never let a failing grade just roll off her back like that, and she said so.

"Well, frankly, it's not going to get any better if you sit home and brood, girl. And don't tell me about that lame French book again. Please."

Julie looked at her picture of Matt.

"Call him in the morning," Dahlia said. "He's not going anywhere. He loves you, Julie. Trust me. Come on—the party's gonna be happening. They're having a DJ and dancing—I promise you'll forget about that Professor Copeface. We'll get all decked out—the two most beautiful roomies at Madison. Listen, even Marion's going. She's spent all week psyching herself up to ask that science nerd to dance with her. Besides, you know you're dying for someplace to wear that beaded dress."

Julie smiled. When Dahlia got started, it was hard to say no to her. Besides, it would be kind of fun to get all dressed up and make a big deal of going out. She liked to do it at home with Matt, so why not at school? She got up and went over to the telephone. "Okay. You've convinced me. Just let me try Matt once more."

Dahlia jumped up and put her hand over the telephone. "Why? So you can miss him even more? Julie, there are still eight weeks till vacation, and then the rest of the year—and the next three. You can't spend all of it calling home, or you might as well pack up and go back there."

Julie frowned. "Are you trying to get me really depressed? I've heard this already today."

"*Au contraire,* girl. I just want to see you go out and have some fun without worrying about Matt for once."

"But I want to worry about Matt," Julie protested. "First Mom and Dad, and now you."

Dahlia put a hand on her hip. "You know, Julie, you're supposed to be the smart one around here. Maybe you fought with Matt because talking with a guy on the phone is no substitute for the real thing. Why don't you get out and live a little?"

"Well, I guess I could wait until tomorrow to call," Julie said uncertainly. Still, there was something in Dahlia's words that rang clear. *Get out and live.* Matt was a firm believer in that. Mary Beth had been, too. "Yeah, of course I can," Julie said with more certainty. "Okay, Dahlia. You win."

Dahlia grinned. "Of course I do. Okay, then. One night without calling Matt, without mentioning Matt, without—well, no, I guess I can't tell you not to think of him, but promise me you'll go out and have fun."

"It's a deal."

"And you'll wear the beaded dress," Dahlia added.

"Definitely."

"Great," Dahlia said. "Then help me plan out what I'm going to wear. Tonight we're gonna turn heads."

"Wanna dance?" asked a tall guy in baggy pants, his T-shirt flashing a rainbow of colors under the revolving mirror ball.

Julie could feel the beat of the music with her

whole body, but she couldn't relax. The guy in front of her was someone she'd never seen before. Ever. And they were supposed to go out on the dance floor and smile at each other and let loose together. Instant friends. "Maybe a little later, okay?" she said.

The guy shrugged. "Sure," he said. "I'll check you out in a bit. Nice dress," he added over the music.

"Thanks." Julie watched him walk away, and search the room for someone else he could dance with. Then she glanced down. Her dress glinted and shone under the lights. Dahlia had lent her a pair of bone-colored sandals with a sculpted heel —a perfect match. She'd swept her hair up off her neck and face, with wispy tendrils coming down in a soft frame, and she'd spent a long time on her makeup. But why had she bothered? She felt like a total wallflower.

It wasn't a feeling she was used to. She might not be as wild as Dahlia, but at home she'd always danced the longest and the hardest, tearing up the floor with Matt and the other guys she was friendly with until the party wound down and the music got softer, when she and Matt would end up in each other's arms.

And while the parties during orientation hadn't been anything to stash away in her memory chest, she hadn't sat on the sidelines, either. But there had been more people she knew at those. Or maybe just fewer people she didn't know. Or maybe she just missed Matt worse than ever.

She nursed a paper cup of dark-colored punch and looked out at the sea of gyrating, rocking people. All the tables and chairs had been removed from the Old Wilder dining hall, and the room was packed with students from all over campus. The whole room seemed to pulse with light and music and motion.

She searched the crowd for a familiar face. Dahlia was easy to spot, dancing in the center of the room with Andy. She was wearing a turquoise Chinese silk dress, and her blond hair was loose and flying out around her. Between songs, she and Andy drew close in a private embrace, as if they were the only two people in the room. It was as if nothing had ever happened between Dahlia and Tim Pike. *"Love the One You're With,"* Julie thought, recalling the song, as they broke into another dance. Was she so old-fashioned for staying true to Matt?

She tapped her sandaled foot to the music, her gaze drifting from one couple to another. There were quite a few people she'd noticed around campus, but plenty of new faces, too. A group of girls she'd seen in the dining hall danced in a line, disco-age style.

Suddenly, Julie caught sight of a couple near the girls, and she felt a beat of surprise. The girl was Marion! She and a short, slightly stocky boy were smiling into each other's face and almost forgetting to dance to the music. That had to be Fred, the boy Marion had been mooning over ever since classes had started. *Wonder of wonders. Marion with a boy!* Julie was happy for her, but she couldn't help feeling even lonelier somehow. Even Marion had met someone special.

"Dance?" said a male voice next to her.

Julie turned around, prepared to repeat her answer of "maybe later." But it was Nicholas, and he was looking extra cute in his faded Levi's. "Hey!" Julie said, a smile stretching across her face. She felt a shot of jittery warmth, and for the briefest moment, she had the sensation of being part of the crowd—a hopeful freshman girl being asked to dance by a good-looking guy.

"You look great," Nicholas said, his eyes taking in her outfit.

"Thanks." Julie was glad the lighting made it impossible for him to see her blush. She felt a little silly about it, given that their only other conversation had been based on Matt and Allison.

Nicholas looked out at the dance floor, and she realized he was waiting for an answer.

"Sure, I'd love to dance," she said. Why not? Nicholas was the perfect partner. Nice, cute—and in love with someone else. She put her punch cup down as she passed the refreshment table, following Nicholas toward the middle of the room.

Julie felt her tension dissolve as she gave in to the driving beat pumping out of the speakers. She spun around once, fast, and wound up face-to-face with Nicholas. He was an excellent dancer, following her movements and easing into new ones for her to borrow. She had a sense of freedom that she hadn't felt since she'd gotten to school.

But the feeling ended suddenly as the fast songs they'd been dancing to gave way to a slow, sexy ballad. Julie watched the couples around them coming together in gently swaying two-somes.

"Punch?" Nicholas suggested, avoiding what could have been an uncomfortable situation.

Julie laughed, moving off the dance floor with him. "If I have any more, I'm gonna float away."

"Yeah, hanging out by the refreshment table. I know the scene," Nicholas said. "I don't know whether it beats Friday night in the library or not." The volume was loud, despite the romantic music, and he was yelling to make himself heard.

"At least you can talk in the library." Julie stood on her toes to answer in his ear. "Even if some people give you dirty looks."

"Hey, how'd that paper you were working on turn out?" Nicholas asked.

Julie felt all the disappointment wash over her again. "Don't ask," she said, making a face. "How about your letter to Allison?"

She knew immediately that it was just as bad a subject. Nicholas shrugged. "Haven't heard back from her," he said.

"Oh," Julie said. "Sorry."

"Matt?" Nicholas inquired politely. Julie thought for a moment, remembering the hard words she and Matt had exchanged. "It's complicated," she said. She knew she had promised Dahlia that she wouldn't talk about Matt that night, but with all the couples close together on the dance floor, she couldn't keep her mind off him. She had a feeling Nicholas would understand. "Nicholas, listen, do you feel like going someplace where it's easier to talk?" she suggested as the DJ went into another slow number.

Nicholas nodded. "Sounds good. How about if we head over to the Rath?"

"Great." Julie looked around for Dahlia to tell

her she was leaving, but her roommate was swaying with Andy, body against body, mouth to mouth.

"Ready when you are," Julie told Nicholas. There was no room there for people without stars in their eyes.

Fourteen

❧

Matt took a damp rag and began wiping down the bar, which was sticky from a night of spilled beer. "Hey, pal, it's time to pack up," he said gently to the puffy-eyed guy still sitting there, resting his chin on his hands. A young guy—probably not too far from Matt's age. Matt took his empty mug and put it in the sink. "Closing time."

The guy picked his head up slowly, as if coming out of a long sleep. "Closing? But I'm waiting for someone. Waiting on a pretty lady." His words were slushy from the alcohol.

Matt looked around the almost empty club. A few men were getting up from a corner table to leave, one couple was already at the door, and another stood joined at the lip, oblivious to the fact that the rest of the party had gone home.

The band had already packed up their equipment and taken off some time earlier.

"I don't think she's here," Matt told the guy at the bar.

He reeled around in his seat like a wobbly, slow-moving top. His mouth was slightly open as he turned back. "I don't get it," he slurred. "She said she'd be right back."

"What does she look like?" Matt asked. "What's her name?"

The guy drew his eyebrows together. *The million-dollar question,* Matt said to himself. There was always at least one straggler like this at the end of the night. "I forget," the guy finally said. "But she's real cute."

Matt shook his head. "I think it's time to go home, pal," he said. He watched the guy struggle to his feet and lumber toward the door. *Sad,* Matt thought, not feeling too happy himself. But at least he wasn't one of those people looking for someone—anyone—to hold on to for a few hours in the disappearing night. Still, Matt felt lonelier than he had since Mark had died in the accident. And Julie seemed so far away at the moment that he found he couldn't even call up an image of her face.

He collected the rest of the empty glasses from the bar. The first couple of weeks, there had been something almost appealingly romantic in their separation—like a young couple in some three-handkerchief movie. But recently, Matt had found himself having doubts about this long-distance thing. Why had Julie been so against the idea of a visit from him? Why had she sounded so strained on the phone? And then there had been the episode with her father that morning. To make the tension worse, Matt had been trying to call Julie all night and she wasn't home.

He glanced at the Budweiser clock on the wall behind the bar. Two A.M. He went over to the phone and dialed Julie's number. His fingers punched the buttons automatically, having memorized the pattern from repeated practice. One ring. Two, three, four. He let it ring and ring, but no one picked up.

"Damn!" he muttered, hanging up the receiver.

"Bad night?" said a girl's voice.

Matt recognized her perfume before he turned around. Traci. "Hey! I thought everyone had left," he said. She had on a black leather vest with nothing under it, and jeans with more rips than fabric. Her auburn hair was in seductive disarray.

Traci looked around the big, empty space, as if confirming Matt's words. "What happened to my ride home?" She frowned. "Jeez. I just went to the ladies' room and he takes off on me."

"Whoops," Matt said, realizing his mistake. "Dark, spiky hair, black T-shirt?"

Traci nodded. "Seen him?"

"I didn't know anybody was still around. I sent the guy home. I'm really sorry, Traci," Matt said. "Although if you ask me, he seemed too drunk to drive."

Traci pouted. "Well, I didn't ask you, Grandma."

"Hey, Trace, don't get mad," Matt said. "The guy didn't even remember your name. You deserve better than that."

Traci slumped down on one of the bar stools. "Maybe. But at least I would have had a way to get home. I mean, Tina just split on me without even telling me."

"I'll give you a lift," Matt assured her. "It's the least I can do. You're gonna have to wait until I finish cleaning up, though."

Traci's mood picked up immediately. "No prob. I'll help. Toss me another one of those cloths, will you?" She flashed Matt a big smile. "I remember when we used to do this together all the time. Sometimes we never actually made it out of here, remember?"

Matt tossed her a dishrag. "One time," he

said, his cheeks hot. He kept his eyes away from the door to the back-room office where they'd spent the night, and went to work washing glasses.

Traci flipped on the radio at the end of the bar and started wiping down the tables. It was a familiar feeling. Without even discussing it, each of them did their particular jobs the way they'd done a long time ago, when they were together.

When she was finished, Traci stretched across the bar to throw her dishrag in the sink. Matt tried not to notice how little her vest covered when she leaned over like that. "I'm done, too," he said, turning away. "I just have to make one phone call, and then we can split." He dialed Julie's number again. Again it rang and rang. Where was she? Whom was she out with? He slammed the receiver down in its cradle.

"Let's get out of here," he said to Traci.

"Ready when you are," she answered.

Two twenty in the morning. *Where is he?* Julie wondered frantically. No answer at the club. At his house, only the mechanical click of the answering machine going on. When Matt was home, he picked right up on his bedroom extension. Now, the taped voice of his father asked Julie to leave a message and the time she was calling. Julie hung up, embarrassed to be calling in the middle of the night.

If only she had kept her promise to Dahlia and waited until the next day to call. Then she wouldn't have had to worry about what Matt was doing out at that hour. She felt queasy and nervous, and her heart was racing. Was Matt with someone else?

Over a soda at the Rathskeller, Nicholas had confided that he was afraid he and Allison wouldn't last. He was worried that Allison was seeing another guy. It did seem as though Nicholas did most of the calling and writing, still feeling a little amazed that he'd gotten together with his dream girl after all that time. Julie wondered whether maybe he was so busy mooning over Allison that he hadn't gotten around to considering whether they were really right for each other.

But Julie hadn't voiced any of her doubts. There was no question that Nicholas's longing, at least, was real. And Julie knew about that. She knew what it was like to dream about someone who was far away. She just hoped she wasn't fooling herself about her relationship, the way she suspected Nicholas might be doing.

Julie stared at the silent phone, as if it could give her some answer. Maybe if she held her breath and counted to a hundred, it would ring and she'd hear Matt's voice and all her worries would melt away. She made it to forty-five, inhaling a big gasp of air as she flopped down on her bed. *Don't be such a moron,* she told herself. *Playing superstitious games isn't going to solve anything.*

She unzipped the beaded dress and started getting ready for bed. The only thing to do was to go to sleep. In the morning, she'd try Matt again. He was probably just out with Steven. Yeah, that was it. Boys' night out. Nothing for Julie to worry about.

Matt stopped his motorcycle in front of Traci's house. She unclasped her arms from around his waist and got off, letting one hand drift to his shoulder. "Why don't you come in?" she asked easily.

Matt sat on his Harley, the motor still running.

"Hey, it beats going home and listening to her phone ring all night," Traci added. Matt looked up in surprise. He'd forgotten that Traci noticed a lot more than she let on sometimes. "Come on. I'll make you a sandwich or something," she said. "You still like a late-night snack, don't you?"

Matt cut the engine. "Yeah, I do," he said. And it was true—he couldn't face Julie's phone ringing and ringing in his ear anymore. Hell, if she could be out at two thirty in the morning, so could he.

He followed Traci inside her parents' sprawling ranch-style house. He knew just how it was going to look inside, from the floral print sofa with the matching curtains to the framed photos of Traci's grown-up brother and sister and their families. *Should I be here at all?* Matt wondered nervously, watching Traci take off the light sweater she'd put on over her vest and throw it on the armchair.

A scraggly little gray dog waddled into the room. "Hi, Sparky," Matt said shakily, stooping to scratch Sparky's head.

"Make yourself comfortable. My folks are sound asleep on the other side of the house." Traci touched Matt's cheek. "Hey, you're trembling!" she said.

It was true. Even though it was warm in Traci's house, Matt was shivering. He let Traci take him by the hand and lead him over to the couch. She sat him down and began to massage his shoulder blades. He felt the knots of tension under her fingers.

"Wow!" she exclaimed, kneading out the tightness with a firm, circling motion of her fingers. "Too much work, Matt. Too much worrying. Just let yourself relax, honey."

Matt breathed deeply, trying to let go of all his thoughts. Traci's hands on his back felt wonderful, releasing all the strain of the last few days. She worked her way down his spine. Then up again. He could smell her perfume, feel her nearness and the warmth of her skin. The deep, massaging motion gave way to a soft, soothing stroking. He felt her moist lips touch the curve where his neck met his shoulders.

He didn't respond. But he didn't tell her to stop, either. It felt too good. She continued to stroke his back, his neck, his arms. His body tingled. She massaged his hands, his fingers, the muscle in the fleshy V between his thumb and index finger. He hadn't had any idea how much tension he'd been holding in that tiny spot. She brought one hand to her mouth and kissed his palm.

She touched his cheek again, leaning forward till their faces were close together. Her fingers moved to his mouth, tracing the full curve of his lips. Matt drew closer until their lips touched.

He pulled back slightly, then sought her lips again in a deeper kiss. His arms were around her. He felt them falling together down into the plushy cushions of the sofa. He slid his hand down her bare arm, soft and warm. Traci moved her hands over his chest, then moved one of them to the top button of her vest and undid it.

Matt shifted away from Traci as he sat up. An image of Julie was clear in his mind, the image he'd been searching for all night—her deep brown eyes and thick, dark brows, the strong, graceful curve of her nose, her mouth, her smile . . .

"Hey, don't stop," Traci said softly. "It was just getting interesting."

Matt sighed. "Yeah, it was," he agreed. "But it's just not right, Traci. At least not for me." He stood up and tucked in his shirt. "I'm sorry."

Traci got up, too. "You're not going, are you?"

Matt nodded. "I have to," he said, a little reluctantly.

"What about that sandwich?" she asked. Matt could hear the hurt in her voice.

He looked at her. She was as pretty as she'd ever been, and he was so comfortable with her. But he knew he had to leave. "I'll take you up on that sandwich another time, Traci, okay? When the temperature between us goes down a little." He leaned forward and gave her a light little kiss on the forehead. " 'Night, Traci. I'm truly sorry if I made you feel bad."

Traci smiled in a what-can-you-do sort of way. "You made me feel awesome. That's the problem." She walked him to the door, rebuttoning the top of her vest. "Matt?"

"Yeah?" Matt paused on her doorstep.

"I hope she's there when you call."

"Me, too," Matt said.

Fifteen

❧

Julie tossed and turned under the covers. She couldn't sleep. Each time she closed her eyes, she'd see Matt and Steven sitting on Steven's front step shooting the breeze, but Steven kept dissolving into the image of some pretty girl or other whom Matt had met at the Fast Lane.

Julie squeezed her eyes shut once more, fighting for sleep. But as soon as she felt herself drifting off she'd think of Matt, and her body would be jolted by a shudder of wakefulness. She pushed off her sheets and went to the phone. Once more. Just one more try. *Please be there,* she hoped silently as she dialed his number. *Please pick up the phone.*

The very first ring was clipped short as he picked up. "Hello?"

"You're home!"

"Jules! I was just staring at the phone, trying to decide if I should try you again. Where've you been?" Matt's voice sounded skittish, nervous.

"I was at a party, then out with a friend. Where've you been?" Julie asked.

"A friend? What friend?" Matt demanded. "Jules, it's three o'clock in the morning."

"I could say the same thing to you," Julie defended herself. "My friend's name is Nicholas." Dead silence on the other end. "Yes, he's a boy," Julie said. "No, nothing happened. Nothing's going to happen." She took a deep breath. All she wanted was to have everything be right between her and Matt, to erase all the suspicious pictures she had in her head and all the tense words of their last conversation. "So, where've you been?"

"At the club," Matt said. "As usual."

Julie felt her heart plunge. "Matt, I tried you there nearly an hour ago." Why hadn't he said he was at Steven's? That was the answer she wanted to hear. That was the answer she would have felt safe with.

There was a brief pause. "I had to give someone a ride home after closing," Matt said stiffly.

"Someone?" Julie asked, holding her breath.

"Traci," he added. "Her ride left without her."

Julie shut her eyes. Traci Clark, his old girlfriend. Why had he said that? Why did he have to say that? Traci was a real party girl, part of the crowd Mary Beth used to hang out with. She and Julie didn't have much in common. Except Matt.

Julie held her breath, expecting Matt to echo her own words about Nicholas: *Nothing happened. Nothing's going to happen.* But Matt was silent. "And then?" she asked tentatively.

"Then . . . nothing," Matt said.

"Nothing?"

"Almost nothing."

Almost! Julie groped her way to the edge of her bed and sank down. She was afraid to think, afraid to feel. "Almost? Matt, what's that supposed to mean?"

It took Matt a long time to answer. "I—kissed her good night. I wish I hadn't."

"A real kiss?" Julie asked, immediately answering her own question. Of course it was a real kiss, or it wouldn't be worth mentioning. "One kiss?"

"More than one," Matt admitted. "But that was all. A few kisses."

Julie was too startled to say anything. She pictured Matt and Traci on Traci's doorstep, kissing. Kissing for real, kissing passionately. Or maybe they hadn't been on her doorstep. She saw them on a couch, on a bed, Traci's auburn hair against the white sheets . . . Julie's throat was tight.

Her whole body was tight, every muscle contracted.

"Is she there now?" Julie clenched the phone receiver as if to squeeze off the bad news.

"Julie, I told you it stopped at a little kissing," Matt said. "I'm alone, I promise."

"So I'm just supposed to act like nothing happened." Julie couldn't get the images out of her head—Matt kissing Traci, running his hands through her hair, Traci with her arms around him, touching him the way Julie did.

"Julie, I didn't mean for it to go that way," Matt insisted. "It didn't mean anything. Really."

"And you have the nerve to grill me about where I've been?" Julie felt numb. "I mean, believe me, if I wanted to find someone else, there are plenty of guys out here." She heard the harshness in her words, but she couldn't help herself. If she could stay true, why couldn't Matt?

"Well, maybe that *is* what you want," Matt snapped back. "You did say you were with some guy named Nicholas."

"I also said nothing happened, Matt. He's a friend. And he has a girlfriend. One he doesn't cheat on." Julie felt the cramping in her chest that came before the tears. "How can you say that I want someone else? You're the one who was with someone else, not me."

"And you're the one who told me not to come out there. Julie, what am I supposed to think? I love you. I want us to be together, and the only thing that's stopping us is you."

Julie felt the tears of anger and hurt starting to work their way down her cheeks. How dare Matt put her on the defensive after what he'd done? "Right, Matt. In love with me, with your arms around her."

Matt was quiet for a long time. "Julie, I don't want to sit here saying things that are going to hurt you even more," he finally said, his voice low. "I apologize. I'm sorry. It will never happen again. All I want is for you to give me a chance to show you how much I love you."

Julie's face was wet, her chest heaving. Matt and Traci. She could see them in her mind's eye, see Traci where her own image should have been. How could she be with Matt when all she could see was those awful pictures in her head?

"Julie, what can I say?" Matt was asking. "What can I do?"

Julie felt herself closing up, shutting herself off from him. "Don't do me any favors, Matt. You've done more than enough already." She didn't want to hear his voice, didn't want to see him in her head—to see him with his arms around another girl. She wanted to be alone. She felt herself moving toward the telephone on her wall.

"Julie." Matt was saying her name. Had he been saying Traci's only a little while earlier? Julie could picture him whispering in Traci's ear. "Julie, please," he repeated. "Julie."

Traci, Julie heard him say in her mind. She slammed the receiver down. Four years, they had thought they would last. Four years staying true to each other. Four years—their love was that strong. Well, they hadn't managed even four weeks. That is, Matt hadn't. Julie threw herself on her bed and cried as if she might never stop.

Julie tried to sink back down into sleep. This dream was too good to end. Matt was kissing her, showering her with soft, tender kisses on the forehead and the cheeks. A touch she knew so well, a scent that made her heady and dizzy. "Mmm," she murmured, snuggling under the warmth of the covers. It felt so wonderful and so real.

But there was something dim and vaguely upsetting at the corners of her memory, something lingering behind the dream of Matt's touch. He kissed her lips, a brief, sweet kiss. He kissed her again, more deeply, and suddenly the memory came flooding back—the awful image. Traci! Traci and Matt.

Julie's eyes flew open. But she didn't see Traci and Matt kissing. She saw only Matt! Real. Live. Matt, looking down at her, his gray eyes full of love. Matt, stroking her cheek. "Matt!" She blinked hard. "Oh, my God! Matt!"

"I had to see you, Julie. Had to make last night go away."

Julie couldn't believe her eyes. But Matt's voice, his nearness, overpowered anything he'd said the night before. She reached up and took his face in her hands. It was warm and slightly rough from not shaving. His cheeks were pink. The pulse in his temples beat under her fingertips. His deep-set eyes, fringed with dark lashes, held hers. This was real. She was awake. But she couldn't be awake. "Matt? What—how—?"

"I couldn't sleep after that horrible call last night," he said. "Couldn't even think of sleeping. I don't know, I just got on my bike, and the next thing I knew, I was crossing the Ohio border." He looked at her nervously. "Is it okay? Should I leave? Should I—"

She kissed away any further words. "Shh, Matt. No words. No more words. Just stay with me, Matt. Be with me." The ugly images of the previous night grew blurry around the edges, breaking up in the potent reality of their kisses. Matt's mouth was soft and hot; their lips, their tongues, exploring.

These were the planes of Matt's face under Julie's fingers, Matt's arms wrapped around her, holding her so firmly yet so gently. This was Matt's smile, his brown hair framed by a halo of early-morning light coming through the window.

Julie kissed the freckle at the corner of his mouth, the plump slope up to his cheek, his eye, his brow. She felt herself tremble slightly as she held him, as if he were a fantasy who might vanish at any moment. She was swept up in the delicious feeling of their bodies being together, her limbs relaxed yet alive, her senses honed on his touch, his scent, the soft sound of their lips, their breathing in the quiet of daybreak, the love in his face. There was no mistaking how she really felt. Here, in person, Julie didn't feel a flicker of doubt. She could see it, feel it, drink it in. Matt loved her, and she loved him. Why had they ever fought? Their nearness made it seem long ago.

Their lips met again. This was all that mattered. Her and Matt, together. Her hands followed the shape of his arms, his shoulders, his chest. Why had she ever said good-bye? To be with him was to be without doubt, without worry. The weeks of longing for him vanished. The phone calls and the loneliness were far away—as long as Julie had him in her arms, as long as she kept kissing him.

His hands descended the curve of her back—down, down . . . He stroked her, caressed her. She found the downy warmth of his stomach, his bare skin soft but taut over firm muscle and rib. She traced the swell of his chest with her fingers, following it with her lips—light, butterfly kisses. His hands slid under the thin T-shirt she slept in, holding her bare breasts, caressing them. She thrilled under his touch.

Their mouths sought each other, her tongue teasing his. His thighs were strong against hers, their bodies pressing together. She heard her own quiet moan of pleasure. Matt was with her. Matt . . . Her fingers found the metal button at the top of his jeans. They undressed each other, slowly, tenderly, exploring each other with kisses.

Julie didn't want to stop herself now. She moved in a kind of heightened dream, with no sense of time or place. There was only Matt and the feel of them together. Just Julie and Matt, and the soft heat of their bodies entwined. She didn't ever want to stop—not if it meant turning away from anything she and Matt could share. She never wanted to turn away from him again, never wanted to be so close to losing him. Every part of her was sensitized, awake to his touch. She wanted more. She loved him so much.

"Don't stop, Matt," she whispered, her words drowned in kisses. It felt so right to be sharing this with Matt. She wanted to be even closer to him, to feel their bodies together, their souls together.

"Are you sure?" Matt whispered.

Julie was sure.

It wasn't the way it was in the movies, so seamless and perfect and easy. First Julie had to get up and sneak into Dahlia's room to borrow the pack of condoms casually tossed on her desk. Dahlia, sleeping snuggled next to Andy, groaned and turned over. Julie held her breath and froze, moving back to her own room only when she heard Dahlia's slow, even breathing again.

When she got back into bed, Julie felt nervous, tentative, shy. Matt kissed her brow, and she giggled shakily. Were they really going to do this, the big event she'd only wondered about and imagined? He kissed her lips and she felt herself responding. Automatically at first, then more consciously, hungrily, feeling the wet warmth of his lips, the delicious pressure of both of them straining to get closer, even nearer . . .

She felt herself slipping back into that timeless trance of pure sensation, pure feeling, following her body's desires—and Matt's. She wanted to be one with him, needed to be.

Afterward, she lay amazed, her head on his chest, feeling his gentle hug. "Did it hurt?" Matt whispered, brushing a strand of hair from her forehead.

"A little. I guess it's normal the first time. But it felt so good at the same time." To share herself with Matt, to feel their bodies united, to find out what she'd waited so long to know—it had really happened. And Matt was really there. One minute Julie had been crying her heart out, and the next she and Matt were in each other's arms. "How did you get in here?" she whispered, feeling a little like he was an angel who had flown in her window. "Did Dahlia let you in? She's with Andy, isn't she?"

Matt just laughed softly. "Who?"

Julie laughed, too. She felt so happy, she thought she might burst. "I can't believe this is happening. Matt, I can't believe you're here."

"I'm here," he whispered, kissing the top of her head.

"Matt, I love you," Julie said.

"I love you, too, Julie Miller. I love you and I always will."

Julie and Matt made love again, then they drifted off into a peaceful sleep.

Sixteen

❧

It was a beautiful day. Dahlia felt the warmth of the sun on her face and knew it was sunny outside even before she opened her eyes. She stretched lazily, moving her body against Andy's. Andy groaned and dove under the pillow. Dahlia burrowed her head next to his and kissed his face. "Morning, sleepyhead," she said.

"No, lemme sleep," Andy mumbled, turning his head.

Dahlia giggled and leaned over to keep kissing him. He looked pretty cute with his face all squinched up. "It's a gorgeous day," she whispered. "You don't want to miss it."

"I don't?" Andy came out from under the pillow and opened one eye to look at the clock. "Dahlia, we didn't go to sleep that long ago," he protested.

"Shh!" Dahlia reminded him, pointing at the door to Julie's room. "The lovebirds."

"Oh, yeah," Andy said. "I didn't dream that. Who is that dude, anyway? Kinda early to be dropping by."

"Julie's Mr. Right. You must have heard her talking about the guy. It's her big-o, number-one topic. Actually, I think it's kind of sweet." Dahlia felt as if the romance was catching. She hugged Andy around the waist, snuggling up close to him. "He must have ridden all night to see her."

Dahlia was certain Julie would be happier now. No question that it was awfully nice waking up with someone you liked on a perfect day. She moved her head just enough to look out the window, her body still warm against Andy's. It was crisp and clear, with a tang of fall coming through the slightly open window. If she were in New York that day, she'd probably go out for brunch with one of her friends and then go over to the Claremont Stables and rent a horse to ride in Central Park. "Hey, Andy, you know how to ride?" she asked.

"Hmm, horseback riding?" Andy was drifting off again. "Yeah. Haven't done it in years, though," he mumbled.

Dahlia kissed the back of his neck. "How about if we get up and have some breakfast?

Then we can take a drive and try to find a stable," she suggested. "Who knows, maybe we'll find a nice comfy haystack somewhere." She tickled him under his arm.

"Hey, Dahlia, cut it out!" Andy squirmed away. "Look, we'll do whatever you want—just lemme sleep for another ten minutes."

"Oh, okay." Dahlia put her head on the pillow. "But only ten minutes."

"Shh," Andy groaned. There was a knock at the door. "Jeez, now who?" he said. "Go away."

Dahlia got up, grabbed the blanket, and wrapped it around herself. Andy sighed and pulled the sheet up around his neck. Dahlia opened the door a crack. It was Tim! She let herself out of the room and closed the door behind her.

"Hi," she said. Tim looked as handsome as ever in a pair of purple Madison gym shorts and a faded T-shirt, but there was a serious look in his blue-green eyes.

"We gotta talk," he said, without even saying hello.

Dahlia was all too aware of Andy on the other side of the door. "Not now, Tim."

Tim frowned at the door. "Oh," he said.

Dahlia hoped he wasn't mad. But then he had someone else, too. "Listen, how about if we meet

up at the Barn and Grill later tonight?" she said.
"We can talk there." She put a hand on his muscular forearm.

Tim darted a nervous-looking glance down the hall toward Sarah's room and pulled away from her. "That's the trouble. We can't," he said. "There won't be any more meetings at the Barn and Grill."

It could be only one thing. "Your girlfriend found out," Dahlia said.

Tim nodded grimly. "This campus is too small. Cynthia's threatening to move out. My sister's furious. She and Cynthia have gotten really tight lately—like Sarah thinks of her as part of the family, you know? Anyway, if Sarah catches me talking to you, she'll kill me."

So much for it being the perfect morning. "Well, what are we going to do about it?" Dahlia asked.

Tim looked taken aback. "Do? Look, Dahlia, I've been with Cynthia for a long time. I never should have let you pick me up in the first place."

Dahlia felt a spark of anger. "Is that what happened? *I* picked *you* up?"

Tim's jaw tensed. "You did come by football practice uninvited, you know."

"And you were really bummed to see me," Dahlia said acidly. "So bummed you couldn't

keep your hands off me at the Barn and Grill."
Forget this clown, she thought disgustedly. Dahlia
couldn't believe she'd been so blinded by his
body and his handsome face. Besides, with his
expression so tight and mean just then, he didn't
even look so great. Andy was equally cute and a
million times nicer.

"Dahlia, I don't have to stand here and take
this," Tim said. "I didn't even have to come over
here, you know."

"Well, no one's forcing you to stick around,"
Dahlia said. "I certainly have better things to do."
Clutching her blanket, she turned her back on
him. All she wanted was to get back into her
warm bed next to Andy and start the day over
again.

She crossed her fingers that Andy hadn't
heard anything, but when she let herself inside,
he was already dressed. "Hey, where are you going?" she asked nervously, leaning up to reel him
back in with a kiss.

Andy turned his face away. "I don't know, but
I'm not really that psyched about playing second
fiddle to whoever that was." His voice was tight,
angry. It was clear he'd heard every loud, nasty
word that Dahlia and Tim had exchanged.

She swallowed hard. "Andy, he's history. He

doesn't mean a thing." She stood in front of the door, blocking his exit.

"Lemme out, Dahlia." Andy pushed past her.

Dahlia put her arm out as he reached for the doorknob. "What about our ride in the country? It'll be a blast—I promise."

"I'm sure you can find some other guy to go with," Andy said. "I'll see you around."

"Wait! Andy, I don't want some other guy. I mean it. Andy . . ."

"Forget it. It's over, Dahlia. I thought we had something kinda nice going, but I guess it wasn't enough for you." He didn't even give her a backward glance. Dahlia felt her heart sink as he shut the door. *Come back,* she willed him. *Please come back!*

But she was alone. The sun slanting into the room seemed suddenly out of place, the beautiful weather like a cruel tease. Dahlia sank down on her bed, where the sheets were still warm from Andy's body. The day had held such simple promise, but in a matter of minutes it had all come undone. Dumped! And by two guys at once. Dahlia couldn't believe it.

She felt glum and jumpy at the same time. Now what was she going to do? So much for a romantic day with Andy. What was he so mad about, anyway? Was it such a crime to play the field before she decided on that one special guy? That's what college was supposed to be about, wasn't it?

Dahlia got up, very quietly opened the door that separated her part of the room from Julie's, and peeked in. Julie and Matt were nestled together spoon-style, fast asleep. Dahlia felt a wave of envy. They looked so in love. She closed the door silently. Why couldn't she be as happy?

She peered at herself in the little mirror she'd bought in town. Same oval face as always, framed by long blond hair. Same strong, straight nose and full mouth, same big blue eyes—maybe a little sadder than usual. Dahlia frowned at her reflection. It just wasn't fair. She'd been having fun. Why was that so bad? What was wrong with the people at Madison, anyway?

She turned away from the mirror. She just wanted to get away from there, from the dorm, from the whole place. A shopping trip—that was what she needed. Yeah, a new outfit to forget Andy. And another one to forget Tim. She'd just get in her car and go.

She pulled on her jeans, a tank top, and her favorite cowboy boots and grabbed her bag and car keys. It was a gorgeous day, and she wasn't going to let anyone ruin it for her.

* * *

The first thing Julie saw when she opened her eyes was Matt's face. He was propped up on his elbow, looking down at her with a dreamy smile. "Good morning, beautiful," he whispered.

"Matt!" Julie reached up and touched his cheek, remembering the night before. "It really happened, didn't it?" The room was flooded with sunlight. "You're really here."

Matt kissed the side of her face and the top of her head, his lips lingering there as he breathed in the scent of her hair. "You're not mad, are you?" he whispered.

Julie shifted around so that she was looking at him. Mad? For a brief moment, she thought about the kisses Matt and Traci had shared, and the hurt threatened to pierce her happiness. She'd made love to Matt only hours after he'd been in Traci's arms. Was it a huge mistake? She could never go back again, never undo what had happened the night before.

But she looked up at Matt's smile, so broad and real. He was so close. And Traci was so far away. Any image of her was elusive—too weak against the powerful love Julie and Matt had been overcome by. The memories, the sensations were strong and fresh in Julie's mind. It had been no mistake.

"Mad?" she said to Matt. "For what?" She

shook her head. "For making love with me? I wouldn't have done it if I didn't want to." She kissed her fingertips and put them to Matt's lips. "It was wonderful." She felt herself blushing. "Especially the second time."

Matt grinned. "For me, too." He stroked her back. "Actually, I meant for coming out here. I mean, you specifically told me not to come."

Julie rolled her eyes and laughed. All the trouble between them seemed almost as if it had happened to two other people. Well, she *was* a different person now, wasn't she? Every moment of the previous night raced through her head. She'd imagined it so many times before, and finally it had happened! Sure, it had been a little awkward, a little painful, but Julie had felt a sense of wonder and joy through all of it. They were together, as together as two people could possibly be. It was real. It was happening to her. To her and Matt. She felt excited, alive, and exhilarated by love and new experience.

"Mad at you? Matt, if I'm mad about anything, it's that you didn't come out here sooner," she said. "I don't know why I thought it was a bad idea. I'm really sorry. Sometimes I get this whole schedule in my head of how something has to be —like I was going to throw myself into school and then we'd see each other at Thanksgiving. I don't know—I get so caught up in my plans sometimes."

"No kidding." Matt laughed.

"Anyway, I'm glad you didn't listen to me," Julie said. "I never wanted us to be apart in the first place."

"Me neither." Matt kissed her shoulder, then her neck, soft gentle kisses. "Jules?"

"Mmm?"

"I don't want to get on my bike and go back to Philly and be without you again."

Julie clasped her arms around Matt and held on tightly. "I don't want you to, either."

"Then marry me, Julie."

Julie felt a beat of astonishment. She pulled back so she was looking into Matt's eyes. His expression told her he was as serious as he'd ever been about anything. "We said it one way last night. Let's make it official. Why wait any longer?"

"Now?" Julie's voice came out in a startled squeak. "Matt, we can't just run off and get married."

"Why not? People do it all the time."

Julie thought about the emptiness that had overwhelmed her during those weeks without Matt. She never wanted to feel that again. She loved him—that's what the previous night had been about. And yes, she did want to marry him. *Admit it to yourself*, she thought. *Matt is the best thing in the world for you.* "I want to do it, Matt, but where? How?"

"Well, I think you start by saying yes." Matt laughed softly. "We'll take it from there."

Take it from there. It was Matt's motto. And right that moment, Julie was awfully glad of it. If Matt hadn't followed his heart—if he'd stuck to her plan—he wouldn't be there, holding her, loving her. Instead, Julie would be waking up alone, the previous night's fight heavy inside her. Matt had been right to let his feelings for Julie lead him. She never wanted to go so long without him again. She wanted to be with him forever. And wasn't that what marriage meant?

Married. Me, a married woman. It seemed unbelievable, somehow, yet all Julie had to do was say yes. *Married. Marriage.* It sounded so—adult. Julie and Matt married? *Me, married like my mother?* But when Julie forgot about the words and just thought about her feelings for Matt, there was only one answer. She knew she wanted to be with him and that he wanted to be with her. She knew she wanted to share the future with him. With him and only him.

She remembered her mother's words: *puppy love.* Her mother couldn't have been more wrong.

No way was this something Julie would outgrow. Not after two whole years with Matt. And especially not after their night together. Her parents were going to see that this was real, that it was something that was going to last forever.

Forever. Julie and Matt. Holding each other. Being there for each other. No more longing, awful phone calls. No more letters that stood in for the warmth of his touch. Julie took both of Matt's hands in hers. They were warm and trembling. The tenderness in his eyes filled her with happiness. "Yes, Matt," she said. "I'll marry you."

Seventeen

"To the border!" Julie's giddy laughter trailed out behind her as she and Matt raced into the wind. Her arms were tight around Matt's waist, the motorcycle roaring beneath them. Matt. The man she was going to marry. Her husband-to-be. She kept expecting to wake up from a dream.

But all her senses told her she was very much awake, as awake as only being with Matt could make her feel. She was aware of everything at once: the hint of fall behind the sweet warmth of the day, the sound of the air rushing against her helmet, the feel of Matt's firm stomach under her hands, his softly worn shirt, the tight tug of her beaded dress against her legs as she straddled the bike seat, the pale blue of the vast sky, the soft blur of greenery on either side of the road, the landscape rising and dipping more dramatically the farther they got from Madison.

The dotted yellow line in the road whizzed by under them with rapid-fire speed. Were they going to make it in time? They'd been told at the Madison town hall that Maryland was the closest state where they could get married without a twenty-four-hour waiting period. But could they get there before the Riverville town hall closed for the day?

Riverville, Maryland. It sounded so romantic. And their race for the border made it even more exciting. Julie felt like she and Matt were a pair of outlaws bent on making it to the state line. Bonnie and Clyde on a Harley. Not that getting married was exactly like robbing a bank, but somehow, with Matt, getting married had taken on a sense of rebellion. Their love was outside any kind of practical planning. Their love was bigger than that, and Julie was finally declaring it to the world.

It was a decidedly different statement than she was used to making. Different, but right. Right to have woken up in Matt's arms that morning— right to wake up with him every morning, Julie thought. She hugged him tightly as he followed the curves of the road. He covered her hand with his for a moment—a brief gesture with a world of love behind it. Julie was the happiest person on earth.

Of course, her mother and father weren't likely to be overjoyed by her decision to marry Matt. "What about telling our folks?" she yelled to Matt, wishing they never had to do it at all.

She felt Matt shrug. "Tomorrow," he yelled back. "I want today to be for us—just you and me."

Julie felt a rush of relief. That day wasn't about *should* and *shouldn't*—for once in her life. It was about doing exactly what she wanted to do, deep down inside. And what she wanted was to show Matt she was going to love him forever.

Chains of love? Maybe for somebody else. The road was open ahead for her and Matt. Julie had never felt this free in her life.

Perfect. It couldn't have been any more perfect than this, Julie thought. The room was on the second floor of the cozy old Riverville town hall, its quaint exposed rafters and wide floorboards like something out of colonial America. The late afternoon sun poured in through the open windows, and she could hear the river just outside, the hiss and spray of the water rushing over the rocks.

There was an American flag hung on the back

201

wall of the room, a large oak desk in the center, and behind the desk, a heavyset, middle-aged man with bright blue eyes: C. J. Reese, mayor, town clerk, and justice of peace, all rolled up in one. "You two ready?" he asked, his voice solemn but his eyes twinkling.

Julie felt Matt squeeze her hand, his palm warm with nervousness. She turned to look at him—the smile on his full lips, the angle of his cleanly shaven jaw, his broad, strong nose, and a look of overwhelming love in his deep gray eyes. She felt herself shiver with emotion.

"Julie," he said softly, "I want you to know that I take this as seriously as anything I've ever done. I love you so much."

"I love you, too, Matt." They held each other's gaze for a long, private moment.

"Ready?" Matt whispered, echoing Mr. Reese's question.

Julie felt a surge of nerves, her stomach fluttering, her arms and legs tingling, but she knew she was sure. She smiled into Matt's eyes and nodded.

"Ready, sir," he told Mr. Reese.

"All right, then. Let's get the deputy mayor in here, since you kids will need a witness. Have to make things legal," Mr. Reese said, heaving himself out of his chair and passing Julie and Matt to lean his hefty frame out the door. "Tom?"

Tom Crenshaw, whom they'd met on the way in, was tall and gangly, and probably not all that much older than she and Matt were. He came through the door holding two red roses. "My wife and I got married just last year," he said, as if explaining his sentimental gesture. He handed one flower to each of them. "They grow wild out back," he added.

"That's so sweet," Julie said, thanking him. She put her nose to the flower and took a deep breath, more to calm her trembling body than to smell the fragrance.

Tom helped them fasten the flowers—Matt's on the lapel of the vintage jacket he'd bought in Secondhand Rose earlier in the day along with a white button-down shirt and a dark green tie, Julie's on the beaded dress Dahlia had bought her. Never in a million years would she have guessed that it was going to be her wedding dress.

Tom took his place in front of them, by Mr. Reese's side. Mr. Reese cleared his throat. "Okay, let's begin," he said. There was a momentary lull, filled only by the sound of the rushing river outside. But somewhere, in the back of her mind, Julie heard an organ playing the first chords of "Here Comes the Bride."

That was another kind of perfect: the perfect wedding she'd always imagined for herself. With the organ music swelling to the vaulted ceilings of a church, she'd float down the aisle on her father's arm in a billowy white satin dress with dozens of buttons down the back, holding a huge bouquet of pink and white roses. The church would be filled with friends and family—she could almost see Grandma Robin delicately blotting her eyes with a lace handkerchief in the front row. The sunshine outside would be colorfully muted as it poured in through the stained-glass windows, throwing jeweled pools of light at her feet. Matt would be waiting at the other end of the aisle, a smile of nervous excitement on his face, more handsome than ever in his tuxedo, a snowy orchid on his lapel. And as always in Julie's fantasy wedding, right there next to her parents and Matt's father at the front of the church was Mary Beth—smiling and very much alive. Julie sighed, and the storybook image dissolved.

"Julie?" Matt whispered. "You okay?"

Julie looked at Matt in his chinos, crisp white shirt, and vintage tie and jacket. No, it wasn't a tuxedo, but he looked every bit as handsome as the Matt in her church wedding—and maybe even sexier. And how many times that day had Matt told her how beautiful she was in her pale, shimmery beaded dress? "You look like a bride," he'd told her. "My bride." Mr. Reese and Tom stood before them, smiling encouragingly. The room smelled of wood and sun, and the sounds of nature played their own special music.

"Everything's more than okay," Julie whispered back.

And it was. She realized she didn't feel sad about giving up the storybook wedding she'd always thought she'd have. Sure, it would have been lovely. But this was every bit as good. This was good because she felt the power of Matt's love and her own. This was good because it was such a surprise, such a wonderful, joyful surprise. But mostly, this was good because it was real. Matt hadn't let go of her hand for a moment. He clasped it more tightly as Mr. Reese began to speak.

"We are gathered here today to join in holy matrimony, this woman, Julie—" He glanced down at his desk, at the marriage certificate they'd filled out and signed not long before. "Julie Virginia Miller," he continued, with a smile at her, "and this man, Matthew Arthur Collins." Julie gave Matt's hand a little tug.

"Do you have the rings?" Mr. Reese asked.

Matt let go of Julie's hand and reached into his jacket pocket for the wedding rings they'd also bought at Secondhand Rose. In Julie's imaginary church wedding, they were two solid-gold bands. But the rings Matt held in his palm were no less beautiful to her. They'd chosen matching silver rings, slightly burnished by time, each a braid of three smooth bands. "For the past, the present, and the future," Julie had said when they'd picked them out.

"Tom, will you hold the rings, please?" Mr. Reese said. Tom stepped forward to take them. "And now, Matt and Julie, please face each other."

As she looked up into Matt's eyes Julie felt a laugh of pure joy bubble up in her throat. This was it! This was the last moment before she would be a married woman! She and Matt were holding both hands now.

"Do you, Julie, solemnly swear to take this man, Matt, as your lawfully wedded husband?" Mr. Reese asked. "To have and to hold, to love and to cherish, to honor and respect, for richer, for poorer, for better or for worse, through sickness and in health, until death do you part?"

The familiar words had never sounded so eloquent and so poignant. Julie held Matt's eyes. "I do," she promised him. *Yes, I do. Forever, I do.*

"And do you, Matthew, solemnly swear to take this woman, Julie, as your lawfully wedded wife?

To have and to hold, to love and to cherish, to honor and respect, for richer, for poorer, for better or for worse, through sickness and in health, until death do you part?"

"I do," Matt said, not just with his words but with every current that flowed between them.

Mr. Reese motioned for Tom to come forward with the rings. "Julie, please take Matt's ring and place it on the ring finger of his left hand as you repeat after me."

Julie took the ring from Tom, fingering the shiny weave of silver strands. She took Matt's hand, feeling it shake slightly in her own. She positioned the ring at the end of his ring finger.

"With this ring, I thee wed," Mr. Reese said.

"With this ring, I thee wed," Julie repeated. She tried to push the ring onto Matt's finger, but his hand was hot and sticky with nervous perspiration, and the ring got stuck at his knuckle. She felt a split second of panic, as if she'd flubbed her line in a school play.

"Push," Matt whispered. "It's okay." Julie pushed, and they both giggled as the ring slid all the way down.

"Matt, now you. Repeat after me: With this ring, I thee wed."

Matt took Julie's ring from Tom. He pushed it on firmly, keeping hold of her hand so that their rings touched as he spoke the words, "With this ring, I thee wed." He leaned closer. "Past, present, and future, Jules," he whispered. Julie felt a burst of happiness.

"By the power vested in me by the state of Maryland, I now pronounce you husband and wife!"

Julie and Matt melted into a long, tender kiss. She circled her arms around his shoulders. He held her face in his hands. "I love you, Matt," she murmured.

"I love you, Julie." They kissed again.

Julie pulled away, happily embarrassed as the sound of clapping made its way through her cloud of love. "Many, many happy years," Mr. Reese wished them.

"Congratulations!" Tom exclaimed.

They'd done it! They were really married. Really and truly. Forever and ever! Julie found herself grabbing Matt's hands and jumping up and down. Mrs. Collins. No, Ms. Collins. Ms. Miller-Collins. Oh, the heck with it! She and Matt were husband and wife!

"So, where are you kids planning on spending your wedding night?" Mr. Reese asked them.

Julie and Matt looked at each other. Their wedding night! It was all so spur-of-the-moment that Julie hadn't thought past this moment. Matt raised an eyebrow. They both burst out laughing. "Well, sir, to tell you the truth, we don't have the slightest idea."

"I guess I don't have to be back at school until tomorrow," Julie added.

"Hmm, I see. Well, in that case, may I make a suggestion? My cousin's got a few sweet little cabins he rents out up on Pointer's Pond."

"Real scenic spot," Tom put in. "Right on the water."

"Maybe he'd give you two happy newlyweds a special rate. The place is nothing fancy, now," Mr. Reese explained. "Just real cozy—fireplace, little porch, great view. A place to be together."

Julie looked up at Matt's face—at her husband's face. She knew she must look just as radiant as he did. "Sounds perfect," she said. As perfect as any storybook wedding.

Eighteen

❧

"Wait a second! Don't come in yet!" Matt cried to Julie, racing up the porch of the little cottage. She stood on the bottom step and watched him open the door. What was he up to? He dropped the key back into his jacket pocket, and without warning, swooped back down to her and scooped her up in his arms.

"Aahh! Help! Swept off my feet!" Julie's voice echoed across the lake at the foot of the cabin.

"The gallant groom carries his bride over the threshold!" Matt laughed, lifting her up the stairs and bringing her inside. He put her down gently on the other side of the doorway.

Julie spun around slowly. The rustic little room was done in wood and shades of green, making it feel like a forest lair—deep green curtains, grass-green rug, pine dressers, and two dark oak easy chairs with pillows that matched the curtains. The bedspread was dark blue, the bed an enormous oasis that took up most of the room. Deep purple twilight came through the windows; a few lights on the other side of the lake were reflected in the water like the first stars of the night.

"Pretty cozy," Julie said, sprawling out on the king-sized mattress.

"Honeymoon heaven," Matt agreed. He flopped down next to her and kissed her cheek. "Which doesn't mean this lets us out of a real honeymoon, as soon as we can do it."

Julie hugged Matt toward her and snuggled close. "Mmm, what's wrong with this honeymoon?" she murmured. She felt his arms encircle her.

"Absolutely nothing," he said. "In fact, the next honeymoon will be on the water, just like this—but maybe the Mediterranean Sea. How does that sound? Greece, the coast of Italy?"

Julie looked out the window across the lake and pretended they were on an island in the middle of the sea, with a salt breeze blowing into the cabin and the silhouettes of distant mountains rising out of the twilight down the beach. "Nothing to do but read and swim and be together, right?" she said.

"And hike into town once in a while and have a huge lunch on some outdoor patio somewhere," Matt added.

"Definitely. Overlooking orange and lemon groves. Can you smell them, Matt?"

Matt nodded, nuzzling his face into the curve of her neck. "It's gonna happen, Jules. Promise. Maybe at Christmastime, maybe this summer . . ."

Julie sighed happily. "Sounds like total bliss. Well, except for one thing." With a tightening of her body, she felt a reality check setting in.

"Yeah? What?" Matt's voice was still dreamy.

"Well, there's one not-so-minor detail," Julie said. "How are we supposed to pay for our dream honeymoon?"

"Practical as ever," Matt noted. He didn't sound overly concerned. "Listen, Julie, now that we're married, I'm gonna get a job in Madison while you go to school. Or did you think I was going to move out to Ohio and turn into a professional couch potato or something?"

Julie propped herself up on her elbow. *Now that we're married.* Major reality check. "I guess I hadn't thought about it at all until right now." Suddenly, she had visions of Matt moving into her little side of the divided double and just kind of loafing around until she got home from class

212

or the library. "Wow, where are we going to live? What are you going to do? Matt, you just picked up and left your job. What are you going to live on? What are *we* going to live on?" *We.* As in *married.* As in *richer or poorer.* This wasn't Matt's problem, this was their problem. It was official. It was legal. She and Matt were married.

"Shh, Jules," Matt said soothingly. He pulled her back down next to him. "Didn't you hear what I said? I'm going to get a job. We'll find an apartment. Jules, we'll set up a home together—doesn't that make you happy?"

Julie felt her nervousness wane slightly. She and Matt going grocery shopping together at the Madison SuperSaver. She and Matt reading the morning paper over coffee. She and Matt making his special tomato sauce in their new kitchen in their new apartment. Not her parents' house. Not the dorm kitchen. Their house. Her and Matt's house. Of course it made her happy.

But the details were dim. Where was this new home? What kind of job would Matt find to pay the rent? "Matt, the *Madison Herald* is printing an awful lot of stories about the unemployment rate in town and the bad economy and stuff. I mean, not to be Miss Gloom and Doom or anything," she added.

"Mrs. Gloom and Doom," Matt joked, giving

her a little poke in the ribs. "And don't you forget it."

Julie laughed. "Okay. Mrs. G and D. But really, Matt, I'm trying to be serious."

Matt sighed. "Yeah, okay. Look, I don't know any more than you do, Jules, but I know I'll find something. Promise. Have I ever let you down?"

Julie shook her head. Still, for the first time that day, she felt a little unsure about what they'd just done. Maybe it would have been smarter to do a little planning. First get the job and the apartment, and then run off and get married.

But Matt was so optimistic. "Anyway, until I do find something, I've got some money saved up, so don't worry, okay?" he was saying.

"How much?" Julie asked, wondering what apartments in Madison went for.

"Oh, about five hundred dollars," Matt said. "Minus the gas on the trip out and the trip here."

"Minus the rings and the clothes," Julie said. "And the fee for the wedding license and this cabin."

Julie could feel Matt's body tense up next to her. "Okay," he said slowly, "so about three hundred. Boy, we spent a lot of money today."

Julie rolled over on her back and stared at the ceiling. Three hundred dollars. It probably wouldn't even cover a month's rent. The sky was

214

darkening outside, and she felt closed in. How could she and Matt have done something so hasty and so huge without thinking about how their lives would change? They'd married because they wanted to be together—now and in the future. But they hadn't really thought about the future at all, had they?

Matt reached out and took her hand. "Hey, you're not thinking we shouldn't have done this, are you?" he asked softly.

Julie struggled with opposing emotions. "Matt, I want to be with you. To share everything with you. But it's all happening so fast, and—there's no turning back," she said, her voice cracking.

Matt raised himself on one arm so he was looking at her. In the dark room, Julie could just make out the lines of sadness on his face. "Why would we want to?" he asked, cupping her cheek in his hand.

"Because you had a job you really liked. You were doing what you wanted to be doing. You had things set up just right." Julie suddenly felt like crying. What if she had told Matt he could come out and visit? They could have spent a wonderful weekend together, and then he would have gone home, back to Philly, back to his job, and they would have kept going just the way they'd planned.

215

"Yeah, I did like my setup in Philly," Matt said.

"See?" Julie felt herself getting teary.

"Except for one thing. Once you left, I was miserable," Matt said. "Nothing seemed to work anymore."

Julie thought for a moment. It was the same with her. She'd planned everything out for herself perfectly—except that without Matt, all her plans had fallen apart. Would she really wish him back in Philadelphia at that moment? No chance. She felt a small laugh rise to her lips.

Matt knit his eyebrows together. "Wanna let me in on the joke?"

"I'm thinking that sometimes *you're* the practical one," she said. "Even if you don't mean to be. I mean, it was no good for me without you, either." Julie reached up for Matt and drew him down toward her.

"So you're not sorry?" he said.

"Nope." She kissed him gently. "I guess I just have to believe that things will work out."

"They will," Matt said. He kissed her back. "Can we go back to being newlyweds on our honeymoon?" he asked playfully.

"Mmm. I'd like that." The room was as dark as the night sky now. Julie closed her eyes and concentrated on their kisses, the way their bodies fit together, the quickening of her pulse. She felt an electric thrill wherever Matt's hands moved over her. Her worries were melting away under his touch.

Of course they had done the right thing. She kissed him again and again. Of course they had.

"Oh, no! Again?" Julie's laughter echoed down the hall of the dorm as Matt picked her up to carry her across threshold number two. From the cradle of his arms, she reached out and turned the doorknob to her room.

Dahlia looked up from her desk as they came in, a pen poised in her hand. The serious expression on her face froze Julie's laughter. "Oh, hey, Dahlia," she said. The party queen studying? Weird. Julie wiggled out of Matt's arms, feeling as if she and Dahlia had traded places—Julie with the boy, Dahlia with the books. "I know you let Matt in the other night, but let me introduce you guys formally."

Dahlia threw her pen down. "Where have you been?" she spat. "I've been totally panicking about you. Your parents have called three times. I had to keep making up excuses."

Mom and Dad. Dum-de-dum-dum. Sooner or later, Julie was going to have to tell them the news. She looked at Matt and grimaced. Then she looked back at Dahlia, who was still waiting for an answer. "Well, we—went on a little trip."

"A trip. Great. And you couldn't leave me a note or anything?" Dahlia pushed back her chair and stood up angrily.

Julie tried to stay on an even keel. Maybe Dahlia felt a little left out. "Look, I'm sorry if I made you worry, but, hey, you *have* been known to stay out all night, too," she said lightly.

Dahlia's voice was hard. "But you always knew where I was, didn't you?" Julie nodded sheepishly. "You got something on your dress," Dahlia added.

Julie looked down. There was a thick black streak down one of her hips. "Motorcycle grease," she said.

"Great. Out for a joyride, and here I was thinking something awful had happened."

Julie frowned. What was Dahlia so bent out of shape about? It wasn't as if she was exactly the most responsible person in the world herself. What had happened to her just-have-fun attitude? "Come on, Dahlia. I didn't know Matt was coming out here, and then I didn't know we were going to —well . . ." Breaking the news was proving to be harder than she'd thought. She looked toward Matt for encouragement. He smiled but stayed by the door, an unwelcome guest. Julie couldn't blame him.

She looked back at Dahlia. Her arms were folded, challenging Julie to come up with some good explanation. "Dahlia, we did something kind of . . . well, I don't know. You might think it's weird," Julie began.

Dahlia waited. Down the hall, the Grateful Dead pumped out of Scott and Bob's stereo.

Julie took a breath. There was only one way to say it. "Matt and I got married."

Dahlia's face registered disbelief, then utter shock. "You're joking, right?" she asked.

Julie shook her head. She felt herself starting to smile. She couldn't help it. She knew Dahlia was upset with her, but she felt herself getting excited all over again. Married. She and Matt were married.

"No way," Dahlia said flatly.

"Way." Julie couldn't hold back a little giggle.

"Wait a second." Dahlia's blue eyes were huge. "You really aren't kidding."

"No." Julie held out her hand with the braided silver ring. "Wedding band and everything."

Only Dahlia's eyes moved. She took in the wedding ring, looked up at Julie, over at Matt, then back at Julie. "This is crazy," she finally said. Julie felt a flash of disappointment. "This is absolutely nuts."

The disappointment spilled into anger. "Aren't you happy for us? Aren't you going to congratulate us?" Couldn't Dahlia think about someone else's feelings for a change?

Dahlia edged past her. "Congratulations," she said coldly. "By the way, while you were out getting married, I was getting dumped."

Suddenly, it all made sense. No wonder Dahlia was so upset. Julie grabbed her by the arm. "Oh, my God, I had no idea. I'm really sorry," she said. And then, "Tim?"

"Tim. Yeah. And Andy, too."

Both of them? Dumped by two guys at once? Poor Dahlia. But before Julie could utter a word of sympathy, Dahlia had turned on her heel, pushing past Matt and out into the hall.

"But don't feel too sorry for me," she said over her shoulder. "Don't let me ruin your honeymoon." She slammed the door.

Julie sank down on Dahlia's bed. Honeymoon? The honeymoon was suddenly over. Definitely over.

"She always so sweet to you?" Matt asked, coming over to sit next to her.

Julie blew out a long breath. "I guess she really needed to talk and I wasn't around for her."

Matt shook his head. "Jules, we just got married! Don't you think any real friend would take that into consideration?"

Julie felt a pinch of hurt at the truth in Matt's words. She shrugged. "I don't know. Sometimes Dahlia *doesn't* consider. She just acts. She has a way of getting all worked up and doing things without thinking first."

Matt rolled his eyes. "You're too nice, Jules."

"No, really. I mean, in a funny way, you ought to be the first to understand. She's sort of like you, Matt. She does what she feels, you know?" Matt's silence was his response. "You'll get to love her, sweetheart," Julie added, as much to convince herself as Matt.

Matt looked dubious. But before Julie could come up with anything to convince him, there was a shriek from out in the hall. "They what? You're kidding! Oh, wow! That's so incredible!"

Julie started laughing. "Marion. I've told you about her." Within seconds, there was an animated knocking at the door. Julie let her in and immediately found herself in a bear hug.

"I can't believe it!" Marion bubbled, managing to jump up and down without letting Julie out of her grasp. "It's so great! So great! So incredible!" she kept repeating.

"Thanks, Marion," Julie said, laughing. "Wanna meet the lucky guy?"

Marion was suddenly shy, as if it was occurring to her for the first time that Julie's getting married meant there was a strange boy lurking around somewhere. She let go of Julie and stepped inside the room. Matt got up and came toward her.

"Nice to meet you, Marion." He extended his hand.

Marion shook it. "Same," she said. "Um, congratulations." Then she looked back at Julie with a dreamy sigh. "Isn't love wonderful?"

Julie arched an amused eyebrow. "It couldn't be Fred from biology, now, could it?" she teased.

Marion started to blush at the mention of his name. She nodded. "We danced together all night at the Old Wilder party."

"And?" Julie prompted.

"And what?" Marion asked innocently.

Julie laughed. "Did you make a date to see each other again?"

"Well, kind of," Marion said shyly. "There's a lecture on invertebrate pathology over in Kittery in a little while. He said he'd be there . . ."

"Invertebrates, huh? Well, don't pay too much attention," Julie said with a wink.

"I—I won't," Marion stammered. "Anyway, I'm really happy for you guys."

"Thanks," Julie and Matt both said, more or less in unison.

"Glad to finally meet you in person," Matt said. "I've heard a lot about you."

"Yeah, me, too," Marion said. "Oh, I just think it's so great, you guys. . . ." Julie laughed as Marion closed the door after her.

"Invertebrate pathology. Pretty romantic, huh?" Julie joked.

"Sure is. What is invertebrate pathology, anyway?"

Julie shrugged. "Who knows?"

"Well, at least one of your friends is happy for us," Matt said, coming up behind her and circling his arms around her. He paused. "I just hope our folks see it her way, too."

Julie's smile died on her lips. "I just hope," she repeated.

Nineteen

❧

"Okay, so maybe they never approved of us as a couple," Julie said to Matt, eyeing the telephone as if it might lunge off the wall and attack them. "But now that we've made it official, they'll just have to get used to the idea. Right?"

"Uh-huh," Matt said, equally uncertain. "I mean, they'll be happy that you're happy, right?"

Julie lay back in Matt's arms on her bed. Sure. And pigs had wings. She wished this were going to be easier. One good thing, though: What was done was done. She and Matt had each other— no matter what their parents or Dahlia or anyone else thought. Julie took Matt's hand and kissed it. "I guess we have to look at it this way," she said. "The worst that can happen is that they'll be really mad and tell us how much they disapprove.

And since they disapprove already, we have nothing to lose."

Matt laughed. "Does that mean you're volunteering to call first?" He kissed the top of her head, breathing in deeply.

"Wait a minute! I didn't go that far," Julie protested.

"Okay, lemme up, then," Matt said, reaching into his pants pocket as he stood up. "I'll flip you for it."

"Heads," Julie said immediately. It was her luckier side.

Matt tossed a nickel up in the air, catching it with one hand and slapping it down on his opposite forearm. He pulled his hand away, looked down at the coin, and groaned.

"It'll be over faster," Julie consoled him, feeling pretty silly to be relieved about winning herself another few minutes. She was going to be breaking the news soon enough.

"Maybe I can leave a message on the answering machine." Matt gave a dry little smile as he dialed his father's number. But when his body tightened noticeably, Julie knew Mr. Collins had picked up in person. She realized she was holding her breath as she listened to Matt's end of the conversation.

"Dad, hi . . . Take it easy! I'm fine . . .

Ohio." He rolled his eyes. "No, I'm with Madonna. . . . Okay, okay, I'm sorry, Dad. Yes, I'm out here with Julie." There was a long pause on Matt's side. "Yeah, I know," he finally said, his tone more chastened. "Listen, I feel bad. Really. I know it was the busiest night of the week. . . . I know. . . . Yeah, it was irresponsible. You're right, okay? . . . No, maybe I don't deserve to have been made manager." Another pause. "Well, it's not exactly a little visit. . . . Yes . . . Yes, I know I have a job to do. Had," Matt amended. There was another pause. "If you'd let me talk, I'd explain!"

Julie bit her lip. She wished Matt would try to control the level of his voice. Yelling at his father wasn't going to make his father any more receptive to the news. She put her hand on Matt's arm. "Easy," she whispered.

Matt seemed to be composing himself. He took a few deep breaths. When he spoke again, his voice was calmer. "Dad, I've got something to tell you," he said. "About Julie and me." He looked at her and smiled. "We got married yesterday, Dad."

Julie didn't need to hear Mr. Collins's side of the conversation to figure out his reaction. It was enough to watch Matt's smile wilt like a cut flower in the hot sun. "Well, it's too late, Dad," he said flatly. "Besides, what were you going to do about it?"

Julie's chest was tight as she watched Matt's hard expression. "Oh, right. To save me from making the same mistake?" he spit out. "That's totally unfair. I'm old enough to know I love her." Pause. "Well, maybe you and Mom weren't."

Julie groaned. "Matt!" she warned him, shaking her head for him to stop. But he was off and running.

"It's not my fault you couldn't keep your hands off every groupie chick who liked fast cars and fast guys," he was yelling into the phone. "It's too bad that you don't like to hear the truth, Dad. You know, I *was* around to see it—even if most of the time you acted like I wasn't . . . Huh? . . . Yes, that is the way I remember it."

He listened tensely for a moment. "You know, Dad, that's the first thing you've said that I agree with. I see no reason to continue this, either. Fine." He let out a sharp, bitter laugh. "Yes, Dad, it means I quit. Hey, and, Dad? Thanks for the best wishes," he said sarcastically. He slammed the receiver down in its cradle.

Julie got up and put her arms around him, but Matt was stiff and unyielding. "Great wedding gift," he blurted out.

"Give him time," Julie said, trying to console him. "He'll get used to the idea."

"Yeah, sure," Matt said grimly. "I think all he really cares about is who's gonna cover at the club. I should have expected that. Well . . . your turn, Julie. It couldn't be any worse than my dad's reaction."

"Wait. Aren't you going to call your mom, Matt?"

Matt grimaced. "Mom. Yeah, California time. She should just about be sitting down to dinner with her real family." Julie felt a twinge of hurt for him.

"I can just hear it," he went on. " 'Hi, Matt! Big news? Oh, just a minute. Jimmy, eat your string beans. Jill, stop slurping your spaghetti. Excuse me, Matt. What were you saying?' " Matt shook his head. "Why would she really care, anyway? I think I'll just send her a postcard." Matt's expression softened as he glanced at Julie. "Tell her how beautiful my bride was," he added.

"Well, okay." Julie sighed. "I guess I should feel lucky that I've got only one set of parents to deal with." As she went to the phone she felt as if she were moving through water—slowly, pushing against the resistance. She forced herself to dial home, foolishly hoping her parents had taken Tommy out for pizza or something. Two rings.

"Hello?" her mother answered. Julie had a flash of their previous phone call. If that had been bad, this promised to be worse.

"Hi, Mom," she said nervously.

"Julie," Mrs. Miller said tentatively. "Sweetheart, I'm glad you called—and I'm sorry we fought."

"Me, too, Mom," Julie answered.

"Let me get your father on the other line. I know he wants to talk to you, too," her mother said.

Oh, no, Julie thought. Two against one. Her parents against her. "Tom, I've got Julie on the phone," her mother was saying. Julie heard him picking up on the extension. It was Sunday evening—her mother would be reading the newspaper in the living room, and her father would be in his study.

"How's my little girl?" Reverend Miller's voice boomed, with more affection than usual. It was clear that her father, too, was feeling lousy about the fight they'd had.

Julie felt herself open up a little. Maybe she wasn't being fair to her parents. They truly missed her. Her parents might not be the most free-thinking people in the world, but they loved her and wanted her to be happy.

"I'm fine, Daddy. In fact, I'm great," Julie said.

"Good to hear it," her father said. "No more F's, I trust?"

"Daddy, they don't give out grades around here for weekend socializing," Julie joked nervously.

"Well, I'm sure you're making lots of new friends," her mother put in.

Julie sat down on the edge of her bed, next to Matt. "Yeah, as a matter of fact I am." She looked at the braided wedding ring on her left hand. "But actually, right now I'm with an old friend." Silence on the other end.

Then her mother: "An old friend?" Her voice was suddenly edgy.

"Yeah, Matt's out here," Julie answered, trying to sound calm and in control.

"I see." Her father's voice had lost that affectionate softness.

"And how long does he plan on staying?" Her mother's words were equally starched.

Julie put her hand out for Matt to take. His touch made her feel more steady. "Mom, Dad, I have something to tell you," she said formally. Her parents waited silently. She could almost hear the tension crackling through the phone line. *Here goes,* she thought, squeezing Matt's hand. "Matt and I have—gotten married."

A matched set of gasps came through the receiver. Then her mother's hushed, horrified voice. "Tell me this is some sort of silly joke, Julie."

"It's not." Julie shook her head. "I love Matt and I want to be with him. I told you that before, and you didn't believe me."

When her mother spoke again, her voice trembled. "Julie, marriage is supposed to be a permanent decision. Don't you understand?"

"I know—*we* know—what we did. We both know what we want," Julie told her.

"You don't know anything of the sort." Her father's voice was low and angry. "You're barely more than a child, Julie. A child who wants to play at being grown up."

Julie opened her mouth to protest, but her mother was voicing her own disfavor. "How could you do this to us, Julie? How? You've always been so levelheaded. We've always felt we could count on you to do what was right."

"You mean what *you* thought was right," Julie defended herself. "What I thought you wanted me to do. What I was supposed to do. Well, I finally did something that *I* wanted to do. For me. Not because it was expected of me."

There followed a long, awful moment during which no one said a thing. It was even worse than hearing her parents chastise her. Her mother broke the silence. "So you're saying that all along we've been making you do things that you don't really want to do, is that it?" she asked, her voice a mixture of hurt and anger.

"No. No, that's not what I meant."

"Then what did you mean?" her father pressed.

No, her parents had never actually forced her to do anything. But somehow she'd always known what they expected of her. Always known, and always done it, without questioning and without arguing about it. She'd gotten good grades in school, always made it home by the right time, had the right friends. And most important, she hadn't done anything that could get her into trouble the way—well, the way Mary Beth might have done.

"You know," she said tightly, "the only thing I ever did that you disapproved of was to fall in love with Matt."

"So you married him because it was the one thing your mother and I objected to? Is that it?" Once again, her father seemed to twist her words around so that she wasn't even sure what she meant anymore.

"That's not it at all," Julie protested. "I did what I thought was right for me and Matt."

"Julie, I feel so far away from you right now," her mother said in a teary voice.

Julie swallowed hard. "I feel far away from you, too, Mom. I feel like you're not listening to anything I'm saying. Don't you understand that I love Matt? That he makes me happy? Isn't that what you want for me?"

Reverend Miller was suddenly the voice of reason. "Of course it's what your mother and I want for you, Julie. But being married is more than just—just sharing the same bed with someone," he said, as if giving a sermon up on the pulpit. "It's saying you're an adult, ready to make your own decisions, and ready to take on all the obligations and responsibilities that go with that."

Julie felt herself let down her guard just a little. Was her father starting to come around? "Well, I think I am ready, Daddy. I mean, we are. Matt's going to get a job and we'll find an apartment."

"And school?"

"What about school?" Julie wasn't sure what he meant. "You didn't think I was going to drop out, did you?" Didn't her parents understand anything? "I'm going to keep on doing exactly what I was doing—but I'm going to be happier about it."

"Julie, I wish I could believe that," her father said. "But real life doesn't work that way." Work what way? What was he talking about? Julie could hear her father sigh into the phone. "I have the feeling there are things you haven't even begun to think about, Julie. Responsibilities you're in no position to handle."

Julie furrowed her brow. What responsibilities? She felt a flutter of nerves in the pit of her stomach. "For example, have you thought about how you're going to pay next semester's tuition bill?" her father asked, dropping the bombshell.

Julie felt as if she'd had the wind knocked out of her. "Tuition?"

"Sweetheart," her mother said sadly, "what your father's saying is that you've made a decision to live on your own, with your—husband. Certainly you can't expect us to support you now."

Suddenly, Julie really did feel like a child. What had she expected? *Hey, Mom and Dad, I want to be on my own. I've got my own family now, except would you keep sending me that terribly, extremely large check for college, which you've been putting aside money for ever since I was a baby?*

"I really don't know how we'll manage that," she admitted miserably. It hadn't even occurred to her! "But we will manage," she added, wishing she sounded more sure of it.

"Well, we wish you all the luck in the world

figuring it out," her father said, his sternness not fully masking the underlying hurt in his voice.

The silence that followed was almost unbearable.

"Julie, this is a real blow to us," her mother finally said. "I think maybe we all need a chance to get used to it."

Julie was crying now. "Okay," she managed to get out. "I'll call when we find an apartment. Is that—okay? I can still call you, can't I?"

She could hear that her mother was crying, too. "Of course it is, Julie."

"We're still your family," her father said, his voice tired. "We always will be."

As soon as they'd said good-bye Julie felt the floodgates open. Heaving in great gulps of air, she sobbed on Matt's chest.

"Hey, hey. Shh," he said, stroking her hair and kissing her softly. "It's okay, Julie. It's gonna be okay."

Eventually, her sobs subsided, and she began to breathe more normally. Matt took her face in his hands and held her gaze. "It didn't sound so bad, babe, really it didn't." And then: "What was it that you don't know how we'll manage?"

This brought on a fresh flood of tears. After a while Julie got out an answer, punctuated by crying. "Matt, my parents aren't going to pay for college anymore. Do you realize how much the tuition here is? It's almost enough to buy a house!" She thought about Matt's three hundred dollars; it seemed like a cruel joke.

Matt's face had drained of color. "I wish I could tell you this isn't scary," he said. It was clear that he hadn't thought about Julie's tuition, either. "But, Julie, people have gotten married in college before. I'm sure we're not the first."

"Matt, if we don't figure something out, I'm not going to be in college anymore." Julie realized that getting married had been a kind of real-life dream. Now she was waking up.

"Listen, I promise you we'll come up with a solution, Julie. You have my word." Matt pulled her toward him and held her close. "I just don't want you to be sorry we did this."

Julie pulled back enough so she could look into his eyes. Matt was crying, too. She kissed his tear-streaked face; it tasted of salt. His eyelids fluttered softly, moistly, under her lips. His cheeks were wet. Her kisses followed the trails of his tears. Their mouths met. If she had to find solutions to life's problems, there was no one she wanted to do it with more.

When all Matt's tears had been kissed away, Julie kissed him once more, deeply and passionately. "I'd marry you again right now," she said.

236

* * *

"So, what'd you think?" Fred asked as he and Marion filed out of the Kittery lecture hall with the rest of the science crowd.

"Really interesting," Marion said dreamily. She hadn't heard a word about invertebrate pathology, but it was the most fascinating lecture she'd ever attended. She'd spent most of it sneaking glances at Fred's profile and daydreaming about running off and marrying him, the way Julie and Matt had done.

Of course there were a few problems to get worked out first—number one being how to get Fred to kiss her. Did she dare take his hand as they walked across campus toward their dorms? Would they stop under the stars in North Quad and stare into each other's eyes, leaning closer, closer until their lips finally met?

Pretending to be jostled by a girl pushing past them to the exit, Marion let her arm brush Fred's. Their fingers met in the briefest touch. She felt the goose bumps rising on her skin. She longed for Fred to clasp her hand. But she felt his arm go stiff, as if he had no idea what to do next. She dropped her hand to her side with a little sigh.

"Is everything okay?" Fred asked, holding the door for her.

Marion stepped out into the cool night. The sky was an unbroken black. So much for kissing under the stars. There weren't any. Maybe it was a sign. "Huh? Um, yeah, everything's fine," Marion said, a little dejectedly.

"Just thinking about those poor, diseased earthworms, I bet," Fred said. "Hearing about them makes you want to tuck them into a little bed and feed them tea and toast, right?"

Marion laughed. She liked being with Fred. But when was he going to start getting more romantic? They'd certainly been spending enough time together lately. She paused outside Kittery. "Fred?" She turned toward him, tilting her head up, her face almost touching his. In the lights from Kittery, their eyes held each other. She could feel his nearness with every nerve in her body and smell his soapy, after-shave smell.

"Yes?" Fred whispered, but he didn't draw closer.

Just do it, Marion told herself. But something was holding her back. What if Fred only liked her as a friend? What if that was why he hadn't made the first move? He'd had plenty of chances.

Marion felt her shoulders sag. "Oh, nothing," she said. She shifted away from him, taking a few steps in the direction of North Campus.

Fred followed, hurrying a little to keep up. "Are you sure there's nothing wrong?" he asked.

Marion slowed down and shook her head. *Maybe it's me,* she thought. *Maybe I need some glamor lessons from Dahlia or something.* She'd spent a long time choosing the right blouse to go with her favorite baggy jeans, but she suddenly felt frumpy. Why should she even assume Fred wanted to kiss her?

Marion thought about Julie. She was married. A wife. One half of forever and ever. And then there was Dahlia, who had half the guys on campus chasing her. And Marion's own roommate, shy and quiet as she was, was starting to see someone. "A cellist, from the conservatory," Susan had confided excitedly to Marion. Her parents might not be too thrilled about it, but then again, they didn't have to know. Meanwhile, Marion couldn't even get Fred to kiss her, let alone marry her.

"You know my friend Julie who lives next door?" Marion asked, looking to fill in the silence that had settled between them as they walked across the campus.

Fred nodded. "You introduced me to her in the snack bar one day."

"Yeah. She eloped this weekend. She and her boyfriend—her husband now."

"No way!"

Marion felt a smile stretching across her face despite her uncertainty about Fred. "I'm serious," she answered. There was no question about it. It was big news. Enormous news.

"That girl with the long brown hair?" Fred's voice rang with astonishment. "She got *married*?"

Marion giggled, nodding.

"Like from this day forward, all the days of our lives?"

"Something like that."

"Wow." They had arrived at the back door of Wilson. "Well, um, give her my congratulations," Fred said.

"I will." Shifting from one sneaker to the other, Marion inched as close to Fred as she dared.

"Well," he said softly.

"Well," she echoed.

He reached out. *He's going to put his arm around me!* Marion thought. She felt a current of excitement pulse through her. Then Fred took her hand and shook it.

"Good night, Marion," he said formally.

Marion couldn't help being disappointed— even though Fred's hand was warm and soft, and even though he held on for a long time. "See you?" she asked.

Fred gave a definitive nod, still holding her

hand in his. "Maybe we can, um, do something next weekend?"

Marion felt a flicker of hope. It was just going to take time. Fred was shy. So was she. "That'd be great," she answered.

"Terrific. Talk to you in lab, okay?"

"Okay." Marion let go of Fred's hand. Maybe next time she'd find the nerve to kiss him.

Dahlia stood outside on North Quad, a hollow feeling in her stomach. Married. Julie was a married woman. Julie had it so together. She was so solid, so sure, that she could say, "This is the man I want to spend my life with." Her whole life! Meanwhile, Dahlia couldn't get it together enough to be with any guy for more than a couple of nights.

She felt weighted down by the starless night sky. She needed a friend now more than ever. But whom could she turn to? Julie was in newly-wed paradise. Even Marion was too busy for her, getting all dreamy about Fred Nerdsky in between bio labs and wondering whether they would hold hands at the science lecture.

Admit it, girl. You're lonely, Dahlia thought. *When you spend most of the weekend doing homework, there's no avoiding the conclusion.* She hadn't had to leave her parents' sky palace to hang out by herself. What timing. What rotten timing. She'd spent nearly the first month of school with Julie while Julie was missing Matt. But now that Dahlia needed some company, Julie was taken.

Dahlia looked across the quad toward Manning, Paul Chase's dorm. *Of course! Chase!* she thought. He had said he'd take her out for a beer at the Rath anytime, and she could definitely use the company. Good old Paul. She headed across the grass quickly. It was nice to have someone around who had adored her forever. Someone she could count on. And it was time to start paying a little more attention to him, she thought. She let herself into his dorm and walked down his hall.

Paul opened his door with a pen in one hand and a cup of coffee in the other. "Study break," Dahlia announced, running a hand through her long, loose hair.

Paul started to grin. But, as if he'd remembered something, the grin gave way to a funny, hurt expression that flitted across his face before settling into a frown. "I'm busy," he said tonelessly. "Too much work."

Dahlia felt her brow furrowing. "Just a little break. Aren't you going to invite me in?"

"Can't."

Dahlia tried to look past him. "You mean you have company?" she asked. Not too likely with his coffee and uncapped pen, but what other explanation was there?

Paul scowled. "That would be what you'd think," he said sourly.

"Excuse me?" Dahlia had never seen Paul like that. At least not with her. "What's with you tonight, Paul?"

"I just wasn't expecting to be blessed by a visit from Princess Dahlia. Couldn't you find someone better to pinch-hit for those other two guys?"

Dahlia pouted. Little school, big grapevine. "If you've heard, don't you think you could be a little nicer to me?"

Paul shook his head and let out a sharp laugh. "Well, excuse me, Dahlia. I've been nice to you since kindergarten. But since we've been here it's like, do I exist? Now, all of a sudden, with Thing One and Thing Two out of the picture, you're like desperate."

Dahlia felt a shudder of anger go through her. "Not so desperate that I need to take this. I thought you were my friend, Paul." She turned on her heel.

"Friend? What would you know about it?" Paul yelled after her. "You can reel 'em in with your fancy car and your great clothes and your megababe act, but so what? I don't know why it took so many years to figure out what everyone on campus knows about you after three weeks."

Dahlia turned and looked over her shoulder. "And what's that?" she asked, knowing she was going to regret asking even as the words were leaving her mouth. But she couldn't walk away without finding out what Paul meant. If people were talking about her, she had to know what they were saying.

"Just that you're totally selfish and spoiled and all you care about is adding notches to your belt —and clothes to your wardrobe. But you've heard it all before, I'm sure."

Dahlia spun back around before Paul could see her tears. She wasn't going to waste them on him. No way. As she beat it down the hall Paul yelled after her.

"Sorry to lay the reality trip on you, Dahlia, but you might as well hear the truth from someone who really knows you."

"Gee, thanks," Dahlia sniffled to herself, without turning around. Was that what people thought of her? That she was nothing but a rich, spoiled kid? All she'd wanted was to have a little fun at college. Now, the tears flowing down her cheeks, she felt as if that might never happen again.

Twenty

❧

Only two weeks earlier, Julie had walked across Walker Bowl alone, on the way to her first class as a college student. She'd been excited, but she'd also been worried about starting a new life four hundred miles away from Matt. So much had changed since that day. Now he was with her as she walked to class, right at her side. Julie felt as though she were starting school all over again, this time as a new woman—a married woman.

It felt a little strange to be walking across campus holding on to her husband's hand while all the other students—the single kids—hustled to class. She wondered whether people would look at her differently once they knew. What would her professors think if they found out she was married? Would Copeland treat her with a little respect, or would he simply chalk up her decision to get married as impulsive, childish, and just plain dumb? That did seem to be the general consensus she and Matt had been getting so far. Didn't anyone understand that they weren't only in love, they were also committed to each other, and they both wanted it to stay that way forever? Her parents, Matt's dad, Dahlia—it hurt even to think about how they all felt. Julie gave Matt's hand an extra-hard squeeze.

"What's that for?" Matt asked.

"Just making sure you're still there for me." Julie felt Matt squeeze back. "Thanks."

"Are you always this nervous before you start classes on Monday morning, Jules? Whose hand did you hold on to when I was back in Philly?"

"Very funny." Julie laughed. "And I'm not nervous."

"Well, that makes one of us," Matt said.

"Okay, you're right. I'm nervous, too," Julie admitted. "It's just that . . ."

"It's just that now you're married to a bum without a job, with no way to pay for your education, food, or a place to live, and with no clue about where to start looking. Yeah, it sounds like reason enough to be nervous."

"All true. Except you're not a bum."

"Thanks for the confidence, Julie. I do love you, Mrs. Whatever-you-decide-your-last-name's-going-to-be. Or Ms. And I promise you that things will work out." Matt patted the little notepad he was carrying. He was expecting to have it filled by the end of the day with information about job openings and cheap apartments.

"Just keep saying that, Matt. The I-love-you part especially. That's the most important." Julie wished she could feel more comfortable about the rest. But at this point, the job, the apartment, and her education were part of one big, foggy dream. The bill for her tuition, on the other hand, was very easy to imagine. *Certainly you can't expect us to support you now.* Her mother's words were still haunting her.

"Julie!" a voice shouted out from behind.

Julie and Matt both turned around. Nicholas was making his way toward them. Julie hoped that he'd have a little more positive response to the wedding news than everyone else. "Hi, Nicholas. How's it going?"

"Hi," he said to Julie. He had a slightly puzzled expression as he looked at Matt. "Nicholas Stone. I don't think we've met," he said politely but a little awkwardly, as if he was checking out the guy Julie was with. He held out his hand.

Julie laughed. "Nicholas, this is the incredible guy I've told you so much about."

Nicholas grinned. "Phew. I was afraid I was

going to have to call Matt myself to warn him about some other guy moving in on him. Nice to meet you, Matt," he said as they shook hands. "You gonna hang with us college kids for a while? I have to warn you, man, we can get pretty dull after a while. Lost to the real world, worrying over philosophy, literature, and what they put in the mashed potatoes."

Matt laughed. "Thanks for the warning, but I think I'm going to tough it out for a little while," he said, glancing at Julie.

"More than a little while," Julie interjected. "Matt and I—well, we sort of ran away and eloped over the weekend. Not sort of. We did."

Nicholas's eyes said he was startled, but his smile said he approved. "Married? Incredible! Congratulations, you guys. You know, I could tell by the way she talked about you, Matt, that you guys would end up together sooner than you both expected."

"But not this soon, huh?" Julie laughed. It was a relief to tell someone who actually seemed happy for them.

"No, definitely not this soon—but I think it's great. A little hard to believe, but it's still great."

"We're having a little trouble believing it, too," Matt said as he put his arm around Julie and pulled her close. "But we're getting there. Hey, it's nice to have someone who's psyched for us."

"It sure is," Julie said. "Practically everybody else thinks we're nuts."

"Why? I bet you two are probably the happiest couple in Ohio, if not the whole Midwest. My advice is not to listen to anyone—you guys know what you're doing. Hey, don't I get to kiss the bride?"

Julie smiled as Nicholas gave her a kiss on the cheek. The three of them started walking toward the front door of Fischer.

"So, how about you and Allison? Things any better?" Julie asked. *Oops. Wrong question,* she realized. One look at Nicholas's face told the whole sad story.

He shook his head. "Let's just say I'm glad that one long-distance relationship has worked out." He bit his lower lip. "We're history. Totally, completely, and finally."

"I'm really sorry, Nicholas." Julie put a sympathetic hand on his shoulder. "But maybe when you guys see each other again . . ."

Nicholas shook his head. "No way. It's really over. And it's better that way. I know it is. Maybe deep down I knew it all along. It just hasn't quite sunk in yet."

"Listen," Julie said sincerely, "anytime you need some company, I'm here for you."

"Me too," Matt said. "You know, except for Julie, I've never met a girl who made any sense. I'll bet you'll get over it sooner than you think." He winked at Julie and she gave him a sock in the arm.

Nicholas smiled. "I think I'm gonna like your husband, Julie. He knows a lot, even if he isn't in college," he joked.

"I didn't marry him for nothing," Julie said as they paused outside Fischer.

"Well, I'd better get to class," Nicholas said. "Welcome to Madison, Matt. Hey, if you want to grab lunch one day this week, I'll show you around after."

"Sounds great. Thanks, Nicholas. Thanks a lot." They shook hands, and then Nicholas headed up the steps. "He's the one you were out with the other night," Matt commented.

Julie felt a tug of tension. "Yeah," she said guardedly.

But Matt smiled. "Nice guy."

"Real nice," Julie said, relieved. "I feel bad for him, but from everything he told me, Allison wasn't his type, really. I just hope he finds someone who's good to him. He deserves somebody special."

Matt drew Julie toward him and hugged her. "Okay, beautiful. Time for school. No late passes just for being married."

Julie held on for an extra few seconds. She wanted to get a dose of love big enough to last a while. She had a full day ahead of her that didn't include Matt. Journalism, French, bio, a shift at the dining hall, homework. "I'll miss you. Good luck. I'll be thinking about you all day."

"Well, just remember to pay attention in class. Especially with Copeland. One F is enough, huh?"

"Matt, don't forget to eat lunch. And remember to tell them how you had a responsible job back in Philly. And make sure not to—"

Matt pressed his lips against Julie's. As he showered her with kisses she realized how much better she felt than she had just a few minutes earlier. Nicholas didn't have any solution to their problems, but it sure felt great knowing he was happy for them. Maybe if enough people were behind them, it would somehow help them work things out. And Nicholas was right; they *were* the happiest couple in the Midwest. Maybe the world.

"Have a good day, sweetheart," she and Matt said in unison as Julie headed up the steps to class.

* * *

So who was she now? Sitting in Professor Copeland's class, Julie had been running all the possibilities through her head again. Mrs. Miller? No, that was her mother's name. Mrs. Collins? That sounded sort of dumb, too. How about Ms. Collins-Miller, or Ms. Miller-Collins?

No matter how many different names she came up with, they all sounded very strange to her. After all, Julie was an eighteen-year-old freshman in a sweatshirt and faded jeans. Even with a wedding ring on her finger, the word *wife* seemed to belong to a different kind of person. A real wife was grown-up. A real wife had a real house and maybe a real job. A real wife picked her kids up from school. A real wife didn't have to worry about her face breaking out if she ate too much greasy food.

As Professor Copeland babbled away about the meaning of investigative journalism, Julie thought about what Matt must be doing. She was nervous for him, knowing he was out there pounding the pavement in an unfamiliar place. She could only imagine the look on a prospective employer's face when Matt announced that he was looking for a job that would pay enough to support a wife and her college education.

The more she thought about their situation,

the more anxious she got. What would a landlord tell Matt when he said that he needed an apartment for his wife and himself? "You're too young to be married." That's probably what he'd say. Julie sighed, afraid he'd be right. Too young, nearly broke, and in love. That pretty much summed it up.

Matt kept telling her not to worry. Worrying wasn't his style. "We know we want to be together," he'd said when they were getting dressed that morning. "We'll just have to make the rest of it work for us."

But Julie couldn't feel so sure. How were they going to pay a college tuition? They'd agreed to save as much money as they could. But how? Save what? They couldn't save what they didn't have.

This was the kind of situation Julie could have pictured her sister getting into one day. Maybe Julie was following more closely in Mary Beth's footsteps than she'd realized.

"Ms. Miller? Ms. Miller?"

Julie blinked as a hand waved back and forth in front of her face.

"That *is* your name, isn't it? Or have you gone back to Miss?" Professor Copeland asked in his typically condescending manner.

"Pardon me, sir, I—I—" Julie stumbled.

"Ms. Miller," he said harshly, "if I were you, I'd think about paying a little more attention in this class from now on. A certain recent assignment that you handed in tells me that you've got a lot to learn before you can call yourself a journalist. You do want to learn journalism, don't you?"

Julie nodded. "Yes, sir."

"Well, young lady, that is what I am here for, so I'd suggest you listen carefully, hmm?" he said, his eyes penetrating as he rapped his hand on Julie's desk.

"Yes, sir. I'm sorry," Julie said meekly. Some things didn't change.

Professor Copeland went back to the front of the classroom and continued the lecture. Julie picked up her pencil and started scribbling down some of the information he had already put on the blackboard.

What if she had flashed her wedding ring under Copeland's nose and shouted, "It's *Mrs.*!" at the top of her lungs? That would have given Copeland something to talk about. And maybe if she had shouted it loudly enough, she'd even start believing that it was true.

Twenty-one

❦

Finally! Julie rushed across North Quad, leaving the school day behind her. Her book bag was heavy over her shoulder, filled with fruit and sandwiches she'd taken for Matt from the dining hall. *Not exactly bringing home the bacon, but something close,* she thought with a laugh. It was strange, the idea of going home to her husband in her little college dorm room. But when she thought of Matt, she simply felt giddy with happiness. She wasn't going back to her room to daydream about him. She didn't have to count off the days until she'd see him. She wasn't rushing home to call his number and hear his voice from far away. For once, she was exactly where she wanted to be—and that was with Matt.

She wondered how his second day in Madison had gone. The previous day hadn't turned up much. Perhaps he'd finally gotten a lead on a job. Or on an apartment that would be their first home together. She unlocked the back door of Wilson and raced down her hall.

She felt a tremor of worry at the thought of Matt and Dahlia in the room alone together. Were they sitting in stormy silence, as they'd been doing when Julie had gotten home the day before. She'd tried to get Dahlia to warm up, but without even a glimmer of success. Dahlia was too busy feeling sorry for herself. And at work that day Dahlia had pushed her tray through the dinner line with only the briefest nod in Julie's direction.

Julie frowned as she let herself into the room. She found Dahlia alone, staring up at the ceiling. "Hi," Julie said tentatively. She peered into her room, but Matt was nowhere around. She felt a jolt of disappointment.

"Mr. Julie's not home," Dahlia said without moving.

"He has a name, Dahlia."

"Okay, *Matt's* not home, is that better?"

Julie felt her disappointment shifting to anger. "Nice way to greet your roommate at the end of the day," she said. "Did you scare him away or something?"

"For your information, he hasn't come back

256

yet," Dahlia said. "I guess I'll just have to do until he shows up."

"You'll have to do? Do what? Make me feel like I've committed some kind of crime for wanting to be with the person I love?" Julie asked.

Dahlia shrugged. "That's your business," she said. "But it's my business if someone moves in here and no one even bothers to ask me. *I* didn't marry the guy, you know."

"Well, you don't have to worry about putting up with either of us for too long," Julie snapped back. "As soon as we find a place to live we'll both be out of your way."

"Great," Dahlia said sarcastically. "Just pick up and split on me, like everyone else."

Julie blew out a long breath. "Dahlia, I'm not splitting on you—but the way you're acting makes me want to. You know, you're supposed to be my best friend at Madison, and you can't show even an ounce of support for me."

"Me not support you?" Dahlia gave a biting laugh. "You're the one who couldn't care less about what's been going on with me for the last few days. You're the one who's so busy being Mrs. Married that no one else gets a second of her time. You're the one who disappears into her little love nook and shuts the door on me."

"Well, maybe if you tried to be a little nicer, I

wouldn't have to," Julie defended herself. "You could try thinking about somebody besides the fabulous Dahlia Sussman for a minute. I mean, you're lying around feeling sorry for yourself because of Tim and Andy, but did you think about them at all? Maybe Andy actually thought he had something special going with you, and then he winds up finding out that you're collecting boyfriends like—like new jewelry."

Dahlia looked as if Julie had slapped her. "You think you know so much about boys," she lashed back. "You think you're so sensible and responsible. But you run off like some lunatic and get married. You told me yourself your parents are furious at you, and you can't even pay your tuition. And *you're* telling *me* how to act?"

Julie winced at the mention of her parents. How could Dahlia sink so low? Especially after she'd tried to reach out to Dahlia by confiding in her about their problems. "Well, I guess I shouldn't have expected you to understand why Matt and I got married," she said, her voice rising. "You wouldn't know what it means to really be in love with someone. To really make a commitment. The only person in your world is you."

Dahlia sat up, her eyes flashing. "Oh, and you're so busy thinking about everyone else? For the past two days it's been 'Look at my ring' and

258

'Meet my husband' and 'Listen to what Matt and I did this weekend.' No one on this entire hall can talk about anything else anymore."

Julie's face flushed. "Well, maybe everybody else is happy for us. Is that so terrible?" She stormed into her room and slammed the door. Let Dahlia say whatever she wanted. Soon she and Matt would be gone and living in their very own home—she hoped. Julie crossed her fingers.

"I guess she thinks I've stolen her roommate away from her," Matt said to Nicholas over burgers and fries at the Barn and Grill. True to his word, Nicholas had put his books away for the afternoon to make Matt feel a little more at home in Madison. "We've finally gotten past the not speaking stage, but the temperature in that room is still below freezing."

"Honeymoon in Siberia, huh?" Nicholas joked. He took a bite of his burger.

"Really. And they say the Cold War's over," Matt said. "They should come around Wilson. The dorm director wants me out, too. He says I'm not allowed to live there. I can't imagine what kind of jerk would have snitched to him about me." He stabbed a french fry and dunked it in a puddle of ketchup.

"Well, you'll have your own pad soon," Nicholas said.

"I guess." Matt frowned. "I mean, that's what I keep telling Julie."

"But you don't believe it?"

Matt raised his shoulders. "Every place I look, it's the same story. The landlord wants two months' rent, a security deposit, and a reference from my employer. When I tell them I don't have a job because I just moved to town—see ya later, Sam. And as for references from my ex-employer, my dad's so steamed that I'll be lucky if he sends my stuff out here one of these days. If some landlord called him, he'd probably say to shoot first and ask questions later."

"So you gotta get the job first," Nicholas said matter-of-factly.

"Right. Problem is, the off-campus businesses hire only townies and the college wants to hire only students."

Nicholas shook his head. "Yeah, that town-gown thing. Even in this place. Check it out—townies on that side near the bar, Madmen and -women over here or up in the hayloft."

The Barn and Grill was a converted barn, and its balcony seating area had once been a real hayloft. The restaurant still had the feel of a barn, with sawdust on the floors, open spaces, and sturdy wooden tables and booths. Clean, simple, and comfortable, it was a favorite for both the town and campus communities. But it was all high-tops and Doc Martens on one side, work boots and union caps on the other.

"And I don't belong in one place or the other," Matt said. "That about sums it up for me in Madison. I don't know . . . I'm starting to think maybe it was all a mistake—that my coming out here from Philly was just another boneheaded, spur-of-the-moment impulse. Typical Matt Collins. As soon as I get something in my head, I gotta do it. And this time, Julie played along."

"I don't buy it." Nicholas shook his head. "What you and Julie have going is special, and you know it. No mistake about it." Nicholas had a note of longing in his voice.

Matt smiled sympathetically. He knew Nicholas was thinking about Allison. "Yeah. I know Julie and I are lucky." He took the last bite of his burger. Despite all the problems, he and Julie were as much in love as they'd ever been. More. Would Matt want to trade his problems for Nicholas's? No way. Would he want to go back in time and undo what he'd done? Sure, there was a job and a big, rambling house in Philly. But there was real loneliness, too. He didn't belong there, either. Not without Julie.

Nicholas drained his Coke. "Look, the way I see it, job hunting's sort of like going on an archaeological dig. You just keep digging until you start uncovering things."

"Yeah, you're right. I guess I'll just have to deal a while longer. Unemployed, broke, and married," Matt said as the waiter came over to their table to clear their plates.

"Can I get you guys anything else?"

Matt shook his head. "Not for me, thanks." He'd ordered a hamburger instead of a cheeseburger, and water instead of Coke. With his money dwindling fast, every few cents counted.

"I'm buying," Nicholas insisted. "They make great hot fudge sundaes here."

The waiter cleared his throat. "Excuse me," he said. "I don't like to make a habit of eavesdropping on our customers, but it sounds like my wife and I went through a lot of what you're going through now," he said to Matt.

"You mean you're married, too?" Matt was surprised. Tall and athletic-looking, with a twinkle in his blue eyes, the waiter didn't look much older than Matt and Nicholas.

The waiter laughed. "Yeah, that goes with having a wife." He motioned toward the back of the restaurant. Through the open door to the kitchen, Matt could see a blond-haired young woman in a long white apron tossing burgers. "That's Patricia. We've been married almost two years now," he said, smiling.

"Wow, you both look so young," Matt said.

"We got married at the end of our senior year here. We'd been together since we were freshmen. We graduated, got married, and boom—like I just heard you say, we were broke and unemployed."

"So what did you do?" Matt asked, waiting for some clue that would lead to a solution for his problems.

"The first thing we learned was that there are one hundred different ways to cook rice. And then we learned how to clip coupons," he said with a laugh, "so we could afford the rice."

"But how did you guys land jobs off campus if you were students here?" Matt asked. "No one in town here seems to be interested in someone they don't already know."

The waiter laughed. "We did a lot of pounding the pavement but got nowhere. So we figured, why work for someone else when we could work for ourselves? Welcome to Jake and Patricia's Barn and Grill. I'm Jake."

Matt felt his eyes open wide. "This place is yours? But how—I mean if you were broke and everything—"

"Pat's folks helped out a little," Jake said, "and we got a loan, but mostly it was a matter of doing a major amount of serious work. This place was just about ready to be torn down when we bought it. Did all of the renovation ourselves." Jake smiled proudly.

"It's a great place," Matt said. Of course, Jake and Patricia had their families behind them. Families who approved. Matt held back a frown. He'd tried not to let his father's anger get to him, but he couldn't deny that it hurt. And his mom? She ought to be getting his letter soon. Matt had made an effort to share the details of his wedding with her, to share his feelings, but how long had it been since they'd really shared anything person to person, mother to son? Matt felt a touch of envy for Jake and Patricia.

"Glad you like the place," Jake was saying. He seemed to be studying Matt. "Listen, I don't know what you're hoping for as far as work goes, but something tells me you'll take whatever pays the bills at this point."

"I'm about one step away from becoming a traveling encyclopedia salesman," Matt admitted.

"Well, maybe I can save you from going door to door. We're having a super-busy year here so far and we've been talking about hiring someone.

Who knows? If it works out, Pat and I could even have a day off once in a while."

Matt felt as if he'd just hit the winning numbers on a lottery ticket. "Really? That'd be excellent. I managed my dad's club in Philadelphia," he added excitedly. "The Fast Lane. Huge place, with food, live music, drinks. Served a thousand people a night on the weekends."

"Manager, huh?" Jake asked, plates balanced in his hands. "Well, I'm afraid this would be more like waiting on tables, scrubbing pots and pans, flipping burgers when Pat gets wiped out, sweeping floors, and anything else that we can think of."

Matt grinned. "Manager's kind of a fancy title, but I did plenty of that stuff at the Fast Lane."

"Can you fix jukeboxes? This one breaks down every other week, and the kids go crazy."

"I've never tried, but I can fix motorcycles. I could look at it," Matt said.

"Well, I think the whole thing sounds promising," Jake said. "I can't pay you a fortune. In fact, right now minimum wage is about all I can start you at, but meals are free, and you'll definitely make some extra cash in tips."

Minimum wage wasn't going to pay Julie's college tuition, but it was the best offer Matt had gotten—the only offer. And he knew from the

Fast Lane that tips could add up. He extended his hand to Jake. "Sounds good. By the way, my name is Matt Collins, and this is my friend Nicholas Stone. When do I start?"

"Monday sound okay?" Jake asked as they all shook hands.

"Sounds great."

A bell sounded. Patricia had an order ready for her husband. "You'll be getting used to that sound soon enough, Matt. Listen, before you leave, stop back and introduce yourself to Pat. She's the greatest, but I gotta warn you to keep your distance while she's flipping burgers." He grinned.

"Sure," Matt said. "And thanks again, Jake. You're a lifesaver."

"Let's hope it'll be mutual. Some time away from here will be excellent."

Nicholas slapped Matt on the shoulder. "Seems like this is your lucky day, man."

Jake headed back toward the kitchen to pick up his order. "Don't forget to see Pat before you split, Matt. Oh, and hey, I hope you guys still have time for those sundaes," he said over his shoulder. "They're on the house. Vanilla, chocolate, strawberry, or coffee?"

Twenty-two

๛

"Okay, you can look now," Matt said, leading Julie by the hand.

Julie opened her eyes to her first glimpse of her new home. Her first home with Matt. The little place above the thrift shop had nothing in it but a big bouquet of pink tulips. She spun around slowly for a better look while Matt stood next to her, grinning proudly.

There was one airy, central room, and a tiny bedroom just big enough for a double bed and a chest of drawers. There was a small kitchen off to one side of the entrance to the bedroom and a bathroom off to the other. Two large windows in the main space overlooked the Madison green, with its narrow, brick walkways, leafy trees, and quaint gazebo. The window on the kitchen side looked out across South Main Street at the Black

Angus Coffee Shop, Books and Things, and Gibson's Bakery. It was so sweet and cozy, so perfect for two people in love. But Julie couldn't help feeling a knot in her stomach as she looked around.

"What's the matter?" Matt asked softly, the happiness fading from his face. "Don't you like it?"

Julie managed a nod. "Sure I do," she said. "It's wonderful."

Matt frowned. "Too small?"

Julie shook her head. "After my room in Wilson?"

"Then?" Matt prodded.

"Then . . . nothing," Julie said. "I love it. I really do." She managed a little smile. "Nice view, lots of windows. Cool molding around the doors. It's really romantic." She tried to sound upbeat. Matt was in such a good mood about his new job and their new apartment. He'd insisted on carrying her over threshold number three—"Finally, a real home I can bring my bride to," he'd said proudly. How could she spoil it by showing him the tuition bill tucked into the back pocket of her jeans?

She wanted this moment to be everything it should be. The young couple sharing the joy of their first home. Hand in hand they enter. One look and they know it's for them. She spots the fresh flowers he's placed inside and throws her arms around him in a big hug. They gaze into each other's eyes and celebrate their happiness with a kiss.

But the numbers on the tuition bill were so huge.

Matt took Julie's chin in his hand and tilted her face up toward his. "Julie, I think I know you well enough to see that something's wrong. Now, are you going to tell me what it is? If you don't like the place, I'll keep looking."

Julie shrugged. She knew Matt had worked hard to convince Emily Holmes, the lady who owned Secondhand Rose, to rent them the place. He'd even helped her move everything she'd been storing up there down into the basement beneath the store. "Matt, it's not the apartment. The apartment's great. I'm just—well, worried about money, okay?"

Matt sat down on the floor. "Jules, I start work on Monday. Payday is Friday. Plus the first month's rent on this place is free in exchange for us doing a paint job and polishing the floors."

Julie pictured the little apartment bright with fresh paint, its wood floors shiny and new-looking. It really was a nice place. "It's gonna look great," she said as confidently as she could.

"But what? Jules . . ."

She sighed and dug into her pocket. What was the point of putting it off? Matt was going to have to see it sooner or later. She pulled out the folded yellow slip and sat down next to him. "This came in the mail today. Forwarded from my parents." She didn't add that there hadn't even been a note enclosed, but she felt a tightness in her chest as she remembered fishing about in the empty envelope for some other scrap of paper, some word from home, some gesture of warmth. What was missing from the envelope was almost as bad as what was included.

Now Julie watched Matt unfold the slip of paper and study the numbers. His brow creased and his mouth turned down. Then he let out a long, low whistle. "Lotta money," he said, handing the bill back to her.

Julie nodded. It was a rotten way to start out. "It's not even like I've gotten only myself into this," she said, "but I've dragged you in, too." Her words echoed in the empty room.

— Matt put his arm around her. "Hey, Jules, when we were on our way to Maryland, I didn't feel like anyone was dragging me anywhere," he said.

"Yeah, but you didn't know about this." Julie waved the offensive yellow slip around in the air.

Their exuberant chase to the Maryland border seemed so remote. "I should have thought about it before I said I'd marry you."

Matt looked grim. "And then what? You would have turned me down?"

"Well, I wouldn't have stuck you with my college tuition if I'd realized," Julie said.

"Are you saying you wouldn't have married me?" Matt's voice was tight. "That you wish you hadn't married me?"

"It wouldn't have been fair," Julie answered, unable to meet his gaze. It wasn't supposed to be this way. She and Matt should have been checking out the view from their new windows, eagerly inspecting the oven, turning the faucets on and off. Instead, they were staring at a whopping four-figure bill.

"Great. So you're telling me this whole thing is a mistake, is that it?" Matt's hands were clenched.

Julie grew even more tense. "I don't think either of us meant for this to happen," she shot back, poking her finger at the bill.

"Julie, how many times do I have to tell you? We'll work it out."

Julie gritted her teeth in frustration. "You can tell me that all you like. But how will we work it out? When? Saying it's going to be okay doesn't mean it's going to be okay."

Matt pounded his hand on the floor. "Why do you always have to be so negative?"

"I'm not being negative," Julie insisted angrily. "I know your philosophy is to take things as they come, but sometimes you've got to be a little more practical. Maybe you should come down to earth and take a look around, Matt."

Matt jumped to his feet. "I *am* looking around and it looks pretty good to me," he yelled. "But maybe you were expecting a palace of some kind."

Julie felt the angry tears threatening to spill. "It's not about the apartment. Haven't you heard a word I've been saying? It's about the fact that you think our problems are just going to go away!" Her voice bounced off the bare walls.

"You make it sound like I'm just going to sit around and let things happen by themselves!" Matt shouted. "That's not what I'm suggesting for a second. Didn't I go out and get a job? Didn't I find us a place to live? I'm sorry if I don't worry as much as you!" Matt shook his head. "No. I'm not sorry. What am I saying? Was I supposed to turn into somebody else when we got married? Is that what you wanted?"

Tears were now rolling down Julie's cheeks. "I

had no idea what I wanted, Matt. I didn't have a chance to think about it. I mean, it was so sudden. One day marriage was some abstract thing that maybe was in our future, and the next day we were actually married. Boom. Before I even had a chance to start imagining what it was going to be like."

"Boom. Like someone shot you," Matt said. "Great. That makes me feel really terrific about wanting to share my life with you."

"Matt, that's not what I meant," Julie protested. "I'm just saying that maybe we didn't think first. We didn't think it through the way two adults might."

"And now you're regretting it."

Julie was silent. Why did Matt have to make her feel that planning ahead was some kind of crime?

"Fine," he snapped, rising from the floor. "You want some time to think? It's yours. I don't need to stick around if you don't want me to." He strode across the room, taking long, heavy steps.

Julie watched him go toward the door. *Great, Matt. Just run away and ignore the problem,* she thought, still clutching the tuition bill, the paper half crumpled in her hand. But as he reached for the doorknob her anger met a wave of pain. *And now what? He walks out the door?* She could al-

273

ready anticipate the frustration and emptiness that she'd feel—that they'd both feel—as soon as he left. What were they doing? Were they considering giving up just because they'd hit a rough spot?

"Matt, wait . . ."

He turned immediately, as if grabbing on to a line Julie had tossed. He didn't want to leave, and Julie didn't want him to. "Don't go. I *do* want you. Of course I do, Matt. I'm just—scared, okay?"

Matt took a few steps back inside the apartment. He let out a noisy breath, and the anger seemed to go right out of him. "Sure it's okay. I'm scared, too. Maybe I just don't show it as much." He came over and dropped back down next to her on the floor. "Now please, *please* tell me you don't think getting married to me was a mistake."

Julie felt a moment of doubt. She shrugged. "Well, what are we supposed to do about this?" She held up the wrinkled tuition bill.

"Julie, come on," Matt implored. He reached out and touched her cheek. "We haven't even started trying yet. There's gotta be some answer. More loans, more work—maybe they can give us some kind of tuition deferment. You know, like buying a sofa on the layaway plan."

Julie gave a little laugh. "Since when are you

274

the big expert on buying sofas?" She refolded the bill and stuffed it back into her pocket.

Matt shrugged. "Well, I guess we're gonna have to tackle that one, too, huh? But first things first. Monday morning we'll go talk to someone. What do they call it—the guy who takes care of tuition payments and stuff?"

Julie thought for a moment. "Account person? Business manager? Oh, no, I know." She snapped her fingers. "Bursar. We need to go to the bursar's office." She felt a laugh rising in her throat. A real laugh. "Weird word. *Bursar.*"

Matt laughed, too. He repeated the word a few times. "Bursar. Bursar. Bur-sar. Stops meaning anything after a while."

Julie felt all the tension draining out in a rolling, unstoppable belly laugh. "Didn't—mean any —thing to—begin with," she managed to gasp out. All her anger was dissolving, transformed into absurdity.

"Bursar!" She and Matt were helpless against the word, the meaningless syllables mingling with their laughter. Julie took in huge gulps of air. Finally, her laughter subsided into giggles. She caught her breath. "Okay, Matt. First thing Monday, then. We'll go to—" She couldn't even say it again without cracking up.

"Well, the guy made us laugh and we haven't even seen him yet," Matt said.

Julie had a few more giggles left. "Good sign. I feel about a million times better."

"Me, too."

"Wow," Julie said when they'd calmed down. "We just had our first fight as a married couple." She frowned. "Let's not ever have another one."

Matt reached for her hand. "Deal," he said quietly.

"Matt?"

"Yeah?"

"I'm not sorry I married you." She saw the broad smile stretch across Matt's face. "I love you, Matt," she said.

"Love you, too, Jules." He pulled her toward him and kissed her, long and gently.

Julie savored the feel of his lips, the softness of his skin. "And, Matt?" she whispered as they drew apart. "I really do like the apartment. It's got possibilities."

Matt grinned. "Yeah, like if we buy that layaway-plan sofa, right? Where are we gonna put it, anyway?"

Julie looked around. "How about opposite the windows, so you can see the view?"

Matt nodded. "And something on the wall next to it. That poster of Monet's water lilies you have up in the dorm. Or I know—remember that Navajo blanket I brought back from my cross-country trip? That would look sort of cool on the wall, wouldn't it? Maybe we can get dear old Dad to send it out here. It's the least he can do."

"And your stereo, too," Julie said. "One speaker up on the left there, and one on the right."

Pretty soon, they had the whole apartment mentally decorated. It would be simple but inviting, with earthy colors and lots of plants. There would be lots of comfortable chairs and pillows so their friends could come over and hang out. "And the smell of something good cooking in the kitchen," Julie said. "The way a real home is supposed to be. It's going to be really nice." She leaned over and gave Matt a kiss on the cheek.

"I know. And things will work out," Matt promised. His words melted into a dumb grin, and Julie knew they were thinking the same thing.

"Oh, no, don't say it," Julie giggled. "Don't say the *b* word." They fell back onto the floor, laughing.

And then kissing.

A paint-splattered canvas tarp covered the floor of their new apartment. Open cans of paint were everywhere: white for the walls, the palest blue for the ceilings—to bring the sky inside, Julie had suggested.

Sarah Pike had a streak of the paint in her light brown hair. Her roommate Amanda and Marion's roommate, Susan, were already rolling a second coat on the wall opposite the windows. Bob and Scott were doing the bedroom, with Scott doubling as DJ on the boom box he'd brought along.

"Okay," he was saying to Gwendolyn. "I promise, only one more Dead tune—the tape's almost over. Then we can listen to something else." He bobbed his head, his painter's cap barely staying on his wild curls.

Matt and Nicholas, up on ladders they'd borrowed from the college building-and-grounds staff, rolled paint onto the ceilings. Julie paused and looked up at them, her brush in hand. Matt was working carefully and calmly, but Nicholas was attacking the job, covering large areas in record time, the blue paint raining down on him as he worked. *It's as if he's painting away his breakup with Allison,* Julie observed, *whiting it out, cleaning his slate.*

As she dipped her brush into her paint can she sneaked a look into the kitchen. Marion and Fred weren't getting much done in there—just yacking about cutting up a crayfish or something as they stared into each other's eyes. Julie giggled as she went back to applying the gloss-finish paint to the windowsills in careful, even strokes. It was so great of the whole gang to come by and help them.

Well, the whole gang minus Dahlia. Julie frowned to herself, thinking that Dahlia was still sore about their fight. As much as Dahlia might have deserved it, Julie wished she hadn't said some of the things she'd said to her. And it seemed as if Dahlia was sorry, too. Neither of them had come right out with it, but they'd arrived at a kind of unspoken truce in the last few days, going out of their way to be extra polite. *Yes please, no thank you, did you sleep well,* and so on. Dahlia had even stocked the fridge. "Matt must be getting sick of dining-hall seconds," she'd said. But she and Julie were walking on eggshells with each other and they both knew it. Julie missed the easy times they'd had at the beginning of school—shopping, tanning out on North Quad, or talking about guys at two in the morning over a bag of cheese popcorn.

"Hey, goofing off on the job?" said a voice by her ear. She hadn't noticed Matt coming down from his ladder and squatting down next to her. He gave her a kiss on the cheek.

"Hey!" Julie said. "You're done with the first

coat?" She looked up at the ceiling. Nicholas was rolling the final corner.

"Almost," Matt said. "With everyone helping, I bet we'll have the whole place done in a couple of hours. Except for the kitchen, maybe."

Fred and Marion were still paying more attention to each other than to the paint job. "Well, they work slowly, you know," Julie whispered.

Matt laughed. "No kiss yet, huh?"

Julie shook her head. "But maybe slow and steady wins the race."

Matt furrowed his brow. "What race?"

Julie laughed. "Beats me." Over the music, she heard someone knocking at the door. "Come on in," she yelled.

"It's open," Matt added.

Dahlia entered, looking more hesitant than usual. Julie was happy to see her, but she felt uncomfortable, too. "Hi," she said a little unsteadily. She rested her paint brush on the edge of the can and got to her feet.

"Hi, everyone," Dahlia said. She was decidedly nervous, as if she felt she shouldn't be there.

Sarah Pike shot her a cold look. Julie couldn't blame Sarah, but she felt sorry for Dahlia anyway. The action in the room seemed to freeze.

Fortunately, Marion came to the rescue. She pulled herself away from Fred long enough to poke her head out of the kitchen. "Hi, Dahlia!" she almost sang out. Was she ever in a good mood!

Dahlia actually looked grateful for Marion's enthusiasm for once. Julie took her cue from there. "We were wondering when you'd get here!" she said extra brightly. "You know everyone except for Nicholas—up there drip-painting himself."

Dahlia looked up and gave a little wave. A flicker of recognition crossed her face. "Sure. Hi, Nicholas. Julie and I saw you at registration." She arched a significant eyebrow at Julie. Julie winked back, remembering the two of them standing in line and giggling over him—a glimmer of old times.

"Nice to meet you, Dahlia," Nicholas said distractedly, going back to painting away his bruised feelings.

"Hey! Dahlia!" Scott came out waving at her with a paintbrush. "What took ya so long? Stop off downstairs at Secondhand Rose?"

Julie's laugh stopped in her throat as she saw the shadow cross Dahlia's face. "No, Scott, I didn't," Dahlia said darkly.

Julie shot Scott a warning look, but he didn't pick up on it. "That's why this place is such a deal," he went on. "The landlady doesn't need much more bread since Dahlia came to town."

"Can it, Scott," Dahlia said.

"What?" Scott asked. "I'm just kidding around. You know I think you've got some cool threads."

Dahlia scowled. "Threads, bread. Lost in the nineteen sixties. Get a life, Scott," she mumbled under her breath. She turned toward Julie. "Hey, I've got some things down in the car I thought you could use—stuff I don't really need in the dorm. Give me a hand?"

"Sure." Julie smiled. Dahlia was trying. "That's really sweet of you. Back in a sec," she announced to the rest of the gang.

Dahlia followed her out of the apartment and down the steep, narrow staircase that led to the outside door. "You know, I'm really getting sick of people around here acting like I'm majoring in shopping."

"Hey, don't mind Scott," Julie said. "He was just trying to be funny."

"Yeah? Him and everyone else on campus?"

Julie blinked in the bright sunlight. Dahlia's little red car was parked at the curb, with half the contents of her bedroom practically spilling out of the passenger seat—the TV set, the coffee maker, several boxes. "Whoa, you planning on moving in with us?" Julie asked. Dahlia had spent most of orientation waiting for all this to arrive. Why had she suddenly decided to give it away?

"I don't need any of it," Dahlia said staunchly.

Julie gave her a long look. Dahlia's jaw was set, as if she was on some sort of mission. "You want to talk about it?" Julie asked, putting a hand on Dahlia's shoulder.

Dahlia frowned. "I don't want to be the spoiled-rich-kid joke of the campus anymore."

Julie felt a pang of guilt. "Dahlia, I'm sorry for what I said the other day."

Dahlia shook her head, her long blond hair swinging. "It's not just you. Paul made me do some thinking. I mean, I was into having fun, but people did get hurt. And I'm sorry I was such a jerk to you and Matt. I guess I was jealous of him. I was feeling lousy and I wanted you to be there for me."

"Dahlia, I *am* there for you," Julie said. "Count on it."

Dahlia looked uncertain. "We probably won't even see each other now that you're moving out."

"You can come over anytime," Julie assured her.

"Yeah?"

"Of course."

"Okay, and you'll come by the dorm sometimes, too?"

"Deal." Julie gave her a hug. "But listen, I really can't take all your stuff. I mean, you can't give away all your material possessions just because Paul and I said a few dumb things."

But Dahlia's mind was made up. "Julie, I don't need all this junk and I don't want it. You guys have a whole new place to fill, and—well, when I think of how much stuff I have and the fact that you guys don't even know how you're going to pay for school . . ."

"How are you going to watch talk shows before bed?"

"Dorm TV." Dahlia tapped the largest box. "Your wedding dress is in here somewhere. The cleaners got the grease off."

Julie smiled. "Dahlia, you're the best. Don't let anyone tell you otherwise. Thanks."

Dahlia shrugged. "No problem. It'll do until your folks come around and send you some housewarming presents."

Julie inhaled sharply. "You think they will?"

Dahlia nodded. "Give 'em time. I guess we were all pretty surprised about you getting married."

"Shocked is more like it."

"Yeah, well, that, too. Here, start carrying." Dahlia handed Julie the box with the beaded dress, then picked up as much as she could hold.

"Hey, how come you didn't tell me that this Nicholas friend you've been talking to me about is your cutie from registration?"

"I don't know." The big box in her arms, Julie could only approximate a shrug. She turned her head to look at Dahlia. "You know, the poor guy just broke up with his girlfriend from home, and he's pretty bummed. Maybe you could cheer him up."

"Nah. He barely looked at me. Probably heard all the rumors about me."

Julie balanced the box on her knee as she pushed open the door. "Oh, come on, Dahlia."

They started up the stairs. "Besides, he's yours," Dahlia said. "You picked him out at registration."

"Dahlia! He's my friend! *Matt's* mine."

Dahlia laughed. "Yeah, yeah. I know. By the way, happy one-week anniversary."

"Thanks."

"You're welcome. Let's go congratulate your husband." Dahlia went into an off-key chorus of "Happy Anniversary to You." As they entered the freshly painted apartment the whole gang joined in.

Twenty-three

❧

Julie fidgeted nervously as she struggled through Professor Copeland's lecture. Twenty minutes more till the class was over. Then French. Then Matt was picking her up outside Fischer for their meeting with the bursar. The word didn't seem so funny anymore. It felt as though some stranger was going to decide their fate that morning. Julie tried to concentrate on what Copeland was saying. Flunking his course wasn't going to help get her a scholarship.

"So you're tracking down the story of the day. But it involves some highly charged issues. Take, for example, the tension between the college and the town. Let's say two students have been arrested for fighting and disorderly conduct in a bar on Main Street." Professor Copeland scanned the room as if trying to pick out the two culprits.

"The students say a couple of guys from town started it. The townspeople say the students were rude to the bartender, and so on. It's not an unlikely situation."

Julie got the feeling that Professor Copeland was criticizing everyone—students and townies alike.

"Well, everyone's talking about it. Several more fights have broken out because of it. It's big news in a small town. But an exposé would certainly exacerbate all the negative feelings, showing that all parties acted as badly as it's said they did. There are plenty of eyewitnesses, but no one wants to go on record with an account. What do you do?"

"You pay someone to talk," a boy in the back volunteered.

"But you leave out the names," someone else added.

Julie felt a touch of annoyance. Why did Copeland always choose the worst scenarios? Funerals, fights, problems. She found herself raising her hand.

"Ms. Miller?"

"You write a different story altogether," Julie suggested, surprising even herself. Professor Copeland arched an acerbic eyebrow, and she suddenly felt a zing of nerves. What was she doing arguing with him?

"Such as?"

She couldn't back down now. She had to think fast. "Like something about the college kid who tutors his neighbor's little boy, or the family who has a student over for Christmas dinner because she can't go home for the holidays. Something that shows there's a flip side to all the trouble."

Professor Copeland sucked his cheeks in. *Probably too sugar-coated for him,* Julie thought, but for the first time she found she didn't care. She'd stuck up for what she thought. Who was to say that Copeland was always right?

"I see, Ms. Miller. So you're saying you'd give up the big story, the one everyone's abuzz about? The headline story that sells the papers? And you'd write something that would be buried next to the wedding announcements?"

Julie bit her lip. Did he know about her and Matt? Was this Professor Copeland's inimitable way of saying she was a fool for getting married? "Well, yes, that's what I'd do," she said, feeling a bit less certain. "Maybe it wouldn't be the story everyone else was going for. Or even the story I was supposed to write, but it's what I'd want to do."

Copeland said nothing.

"Sir, you say you want us to write something that comes off the page," she explained to him. "Well, how can we do that if we don't believe in what we're writing?"

"Then you're saying you don't have a responsibility to report the important news?" Professor Copeland charged.

Julie felt a tremor of uncertainty. "Someone will report it," she said nervously. "Just not me. Not this story."

"Hmm. Rather interesting point of view, Ms. Miller."

Julie felt a wave of shock go through her. Was that a kernel of praise? Copeland was on to the next person. "Anyone else? Mr. Graham?"

Julie allowed herself a smile of satisfaction. Maybe she'd been learning something lately about making her own decisions—in class and out. She ran her finger over her wedding band. No, she hadn't done what her friends would have done. Nor what her parents wanted her to do, nor what Mary Beth might have done. But she'd done what was right for Julie.

Now if only the bursar would see it that way as well.

"You look gorgeous," Julie told Matt, grabbing on to his tie and pulling him toward her for a kiss.

He was wearing the same outfit he'd worn on their wedding day, only now he had on a pair of shiny wingtip shoes instead of his motorcycle boots.

"On loan from Emily and Secondhand Rose," Matt said, vamping as if on a fashion runway. "She said she wants us to make a good impression this morning."

"Cool. We've got the nicest landlady in the entire world, huh?"

"Really. You look great, too," Matt said as they headed hand in hand toward Walker Main. "But I told you that already this morning."

Julie laughed. "I can stand to hear it again."

The air was crisp, with a few wispy clouds in the sky. The first leaves were just beginning to turn red or yellow. It felt like a perfect college day—real back-to-school weather. Or stay-in-school weather, Julie hoped the bursar would think. She'd been in Madison one month. Her first month. She crossed her fingers that it wouldn't be her last.

"Nervous?" Matt asked.

Julie nodded. "You?" They climbed the steps to Walker Main slowly.

"Yeah."

But one look at the brass door plaque was enough to make them both start giggling.

Bursar's Office, it read. Very official-looking. Very serious.

"Shh!" Julie said, giving Matt a poke as they went inside. "We're responsible adults. Married people, remember?" She gave the woman at the desk in the outside room her most grown-up smile. "Julie Miller. We have an appointment to see the bursar."

"Yes, of course. You can go right in." The woman pointed to another door.

Julie felt herself getting jumpy. She reached for Matt's hand and gave it a hard squeeze. Matt looked at her. "Bursar," he mouthed. They were both smiling as they went inside.

A slender, gray-haired woman stood up from behind a bulky wooden desk and extended her hand. "Ginny Jackson," she said. The nameplate on her desk said *Mrs. Virginia Jackson.*

Julie blinked. She wasn't sure what she'd been expecting, but not a woman. The bursar was a real person all of a sudden, not just a funny word. "Hi," she said with a nervous laugh. "I'm Julie Miller. Well, Julie Miller-Collins now. This is Matt. Collins. Miller-Collins." *Get it together,* Julie told herself.

"Nice to meet you," Mrs. Jackson said pleasantly. "And what can I do for you today?" She settled down into her big chair and indicated two smaller chairs for Julie and Matt.

"Well, Matt and I—we just got married," Julie explained, sitting down stiffly. She felt separated from her own words, as if listening to them with a stranger's ear. Would Mrs. Jackson, too, think they were young and irresponsible?

But Mrs. Jackson smiled. "Congratulations. That's wonderful."

"Thank you." Julie's voice was formal. "It is, but—" She took a deep breath. Matt nodded encouragingly. "Mrs. Jackson, Matt and I are on our own now." The ceremony in Riverville was a sunny but faraway memory, the rush of the stream behind their vows of love a whisper in her mind.

"You mean financially," Mrs. Jackson said.

"Right. And the thing is, we don't know how we're going to manage next semester's tuition." Julie shifted uncomfortably in her chair.

Ginny Jackson frowned. "I see. On your own with two college tuitions to pay."

"Oh, no," Julie said hastily. "Matt's not a student here."

"Although one tuition seems almost as impossible as two right now," Matt added. "If there's some kind of loan we can take out—"

"And if I can get some more hours at my job,

somehow increase my financial aid package . . ." Julie said.

"I wish it were that easy," Mrs. Jackson said, shaking her head. Julie's stomach took a big dip. This was it. She'd thrown away her chance at college when she put on a wedding ring. And her plans to be a news-breaking reporter? Even if Professor Copeland couldn't stop her, this could.

"But let's see what we can do," Mrs. Jackson was saying. "Let's pull up your file on the computer and see what it says." Mrs. Jackson swiveled her chair over to her computer table and began punching buttons.

Julie threw Matt a desperate look. He reached out and patted her leg, but it wasn't much comfort.

"Hmm. Fine record," Mrs. Jackson said. "Yes, but you already have a rather substantial scholarship and a good work-study plan. Do you have a major chosen yet? Sometimes there are funds available for a special area of—hold on a moment. Next semester?"

"Right," Julie said, feeling more nervous than ever. "Is there a problem?"

Mrs. Jackson shook her head. "No, dear. No problem at all. In fact, our records show that your tuition for the year has been paid in full."

Julie couldn't comprehend what Mrs. Jackson

was telling her. "It has? I don't get it. I just spoke to my father last Sunday and . . . I know it wasn't paid then."

Mrs. Jackson hit some more computer keys. "Here it is. Payment was received, let's see . . . Friday."

Julie wrinkled her brow. "But that's impossible. Why would my parents pay my tuition and then forward me the bill?"

Mrs. Jackson studied her computer screen. "Strange. There's no information about the check here. Marilyn?" she called out.

The woman from the outside office poked her head around the door. "Marilyn, do you remember anything about the check for Julie Miller's second-semester tuition?" Mrs. Jackson asked. "I see here it was just paid on Friday."

"Leanne did the accounts receivable last week," Marilyn said. "You'll have to ask her when she comes in."

"I see. Leanne helps us out part-time," Mrs. Jackson explained, "so I'm afraid I can't give you any further information right now. You're sure it was your parents who took care of this?"

Julie and Matt exchanged a long look. None of this made sense. "Who else could it be?" she asked him. "One of your parents?"

Matt frowned. "Just like that? Without even a

phone call? Jules, I haven't even heard from my mother yet. And Dad—come on. Paying for Reverend Miller's daughter's college? I mean, the guy's got some money, but . . ."

"But it's seriously farfetched," Julie agreed. "Well, then it's got to be Mom and Dad." There was no other answer.

Matt was nodding now. "You know, that might be just like your dad. To scare us, teach us a lesson—"

"But really he's still there for me," Julie said. Her confusion was split by a ray of gratefulness. Were her parents starting to accept the news? "That's as nice as the money part—that they sort of said okay, even if they didn't exactly do it in words."

"Well, his daughter doesn't get married every day," Matt said, reaching for Julie's hand.

Julie could feel her smile growing. Her parents were coming around—just like Dahlia had said they would. "Wow, this is the best wedding present we could have gotten!"

"Sure is. Thank you for everything, Mrs. Jackson," Matt said, standing and extending his hand.

"I'm glad there was really nothing to thank me for," she said, shaking their hands. "Good luck, you two. Keep up the good academic work, Julie."

They practically flew down the stairs and outside. Matt grabbed Julie by the waist and spun her up in the air. Julie let out a huge whoop.

"Thank you, Reverend and Mrs. Miller!" Matt said, letting Julie down.

Julie slapped him a high five. "Wow, I feel like all of a sudden it's—I don't know—the first day of the rest of my life!" She gave a happily embarrassed laugh. "Corny, huh?"

"Yeah. But I know exactly how you feel," Matt said. "Job, home, school—everything. And the woman of my dreams!"

Julie took both of Matt's hands. She was giddy and exuberant but also filled with peace. It was just the way she'd felt when she exchanged vows with Matt, when she'd promised to be with him forever. For the first time since that day, she could truly believe their vows, looking into his deep gray eyes and feeling how much love they shared.

In that moment, there was nothing but them. At the same time, Julie was aware of everything around them—the pungent autumn air, the pale gold sunshine, the sound of voices and laughter carrying across campus. And Julie and Matt at the center of it all, holding each other in the most special of gazes. Past, present, and future.

Matt finally reached forward and brushed her cheek with the gentlest, lightest caress. "Well, woman of my dreams, I've gotta make tracks," he said softly. "I have to get changed and get over to the Barn and Grill. I don't want to be late for the first day of the rest of my life."

Julie laughed softly. "Yeah, I've got to hit the trail, too," she said. "I owe it to Mom and Dad to do as well as I can." She leaned up and drew Matt toward her for a big kiss.

"Celebration later?" Matt asked.

"I'll wrap up a couple of pieces of cake at work," Julie said.

"See you at home," Matt said. Julie smiled. Home. Their home. It sounded strange, but wonderful. "Bye, Mrs. Miller-Collins."

Julie felt as perfect as the crisp fall day. "See you, Mr. Miller-Collins," she said.

Don't miss **For Better, for Worse,**
the next book in this dramatic series.

Matt's body tensed. Julie could see his guard go up. She took a deep breath, a huge gulp of air. "I kissed someone else last night."

A sting of hurt flashed in his eyes. There was a beat of silence. "Who?" he asked. The word felt like a punch.

Julie looked away from his pained, searing gaze. "Don't be mad at him for it, Matt. It's my fault, not—not Nick's." Her voice dropped to a whisper as she said his name.

There was a stunned silence. Then a blast of fury as Matt punched his fist into the headboard of their bed. "My friend Nick." He spat out his words bitterly. "How could you? How could he?"

"Matt, you have every reason to be angry," Julie said. "I felt so terrible after you rode off, and he was trying to comfort me."

"He was certainly trying to do *something,*" Matt said harshly.

Julie blinked hard. "Matt, I love you. Don't think for a second that I don't." Matt didn't say anything. He flopped down onto his back. Julie watched him as he stared up at the ceiling, his jaw tight, his neck muscles clenched. "Come on. I'm sorry. I wish it had never happened."

Matt gave an almost imperceptible shake of his head. "This stinks! I'm off in Riverville thinking about the day we got married—promised our love and devotion to each other—and you're here fooling around with one of the only guys I thought I could count on as a friend."

Look out for the new Point Romance
mini series coming soon:

First Comes Love
by Jennifer Baker

Can their happiness last?

When eighteen-year-old college junior Julie Miller
elopes with Matt Collins, a wayward and rebellious
biker, no one has high hopes for a happy ending.
They're penniless, cut off from their parents, homeless
and too young. But no one counts on the strength of
their love for one another and
commitment to their vows.

Four novels, *To Have and To Hold, For Better or
Worse, In Sickness and in Health,* and *Till Death Us Do
Part,* follow Matt and Julie through their first
year of marriage.

Once the honeymoon is over, they have to deal with the
realities of life. Money worries, tensions, jealousies,
illness, accidents, and the most heartbreaking decision
of their lives.

Can their love survive?

Four novels to touch your heart...